I0782179

Knights of the Octagon:
RUMORS

Colleen Snyder

ISBN: 978-1-965352-62-5

FRIDAY NIGHT

Is it done?
Almost. I need to leave the letter.
Don't give me almost. Done or not done?
Done.
Meet back at the dorm. No blood.
I'm not a fool.
You were the last time.
You'll need a new escort.
I know. I have one in mind. I'll summon him.
Excellent. See you soon.

The kitchen wait staff bustled to clear tables. Sizzling steaks passed by the booth. Harried servers wove in between patrons. Hustle, hustle. BB didn't know where to focus.

Leelend passed a card under the table to BB. BB examined it. The card had his picture but a false name, address, and birthdate. BB turned his head sharply and looked at his companion. "What's this?"

Leeland chuckled. "Admittance to the floor show. Gotta

have ID to get in."

BB shook his head. "No. I'm nineteen. If I have to be twenty-one, I'll go home." No one told him about a floor show when his dormmates insisted he come with them for dinner.

Vic laughed, mocking him. "'I'll go home.' Afraid Mommy will find out you're out with the men tonight?" The quarterback popped a gummy in his mouth.

BB stood. "No. Don't want to let my dad or myself down."

Samuel sat back. "Oooo… Afraid Daddy will be disappointed? Maybe Daddy will be proud his son finally grew a backbone." The beefy lineman leaned back in his seat and put his arms on the top of the booth.

BB strode away from the table, ignoring the catcalls from his roommates. He knew accepting the invitation had been a bad idea. BB tipped his head to the bouncer at the door. He debated handing him the ID card but decided not to. What would Jesus do? Walk away and keep going.

The young man halted at the bus stop outside the club. Streetlights cast deep shadows on the sidewalk. Brown bags devoid of their liquor littered the gutter. BB muttered, "Best steaks in town. Riiiight." BB leaned against the bench and speed-dialed home.

His stepmother, Wendy, picked up the phone. "Hey. What'd you forget?"

"My sanity. I need a ride home." BB looked around at the nearly deserted street. Only a few cars parked along the road. Not the hottest establishment in town.

"I'll be there shortly."

"Wendy, can Dad come?" BB paced around in circles and glanced at the club. He saw his roommates pointing and laughing out the window by the booth. "I've already taken…no, wait." BB found his spine. "You come get me. That will be just fine."

Wendy sounded unsure. "I can get Mick."

"No. If it's not a problem, will you get me? I'm at Cloverdale." Certainty flooded him. He'd never been more positive about wanting Wendy to be the one to pick him up. Even though she was only seven years older than BB, she'd married his adoptive father…who was only eight years older than BB. Long, involved story. Lives being saved. Who did the saving? They all did in the end.

"I heard they have good food." Wendy sounded a bit confused.

"Yeah, about that. I'll explain when we get home." BB's tone became dry.

"Be there in twenty minutes."

"I'm at the bus stop out front. KO."

Knight Out. The sign-off for the Knights of the Octagon. Octagon because no one had a round table, and Knights of the Oval sounded weird. A tight band of friends and relations devoted to asking, "What would Jesus do?" and then doing it. Or trying to. Always.

Two women walked past the bus stop. Streetwalkers. BB prayed, *Lord, this night went from fun to all about You. Give me words to say.*

The brunette's eyes narrowed in amusement. "Hey, Sonny. Out kinda late, aren't you?"

The blonde laughed. "Isn't it past your bedtime?"

BB smiled but said nothing. He moved away from the waiting bench to let them sit if they were inclined.

They weren't. The blonde ribbed her friend. "Cat must have his tongue, Tamara. Looks like he's old enough to talk."

Tamara eyed him up and down. "Oh, I don't know, Pritt. Seems awfully young to me. Maybe we should throw him back for an older, more experienced model."

Don't say anything. Smile and let it roll off your back.

Pritt moved in closer to BB. Stale beer and cheap perfume wafted in the air. Neither woman had bathed in a while. Their clothes—what there were of them—were rumpled and faded.

Offer them a ride to the Mission.

Now, there was thought. BB put on his most respectful face. "Do you two want a ride to the Mission House?"

Pritt stepped back. "Oooo…he thinks we need help. I don't see your car."

Tamara stared at BB. Her eyes measured him. "What do you know about Mission House?" She pulled out and lit what BB hoped was a cigarette. He drew in an inconspicuous breath. Yeah. Tobacco.

"I volunteer during the week." BB left it at that. Volunteered with his family. They didn't need to know that at this point. He shifted his weight and leaned his hands on the bench.

"Yeah? Doing what?" Curiosity laced her tone.

"I clean up in the back. Wipe tables. Serve coffee and food. Whatever they need me to do." BB kept his tone even.

"Why?" Still, the suspicion.

BB shrugged. "Because that's what the Lord did. He served."

Pritt threw her head back and laughed. "I knew it. He's one of *those* people."

Tamara shoved her friend. She held BB in her eyes. "College kid, huh? Where's your car?"

"I rode out with friends. Mom is coming to get me."

"Mommy!"

Tamara turned on Pritt. "Shut up. At least he acknowledges he has one." She pointed to the club. "Why are you out here? The show's in there."

"I'm not old enough to watch the floor show."

Tamara sniffed. "Just here for the steaks, right?"

BB smiled. "That's what they told me."

Pritt yawned. "We've got better things to do, Tam. Places to go, people to see. You coming?"

Tamara studied BB for a moment, then seemed to give up. "Yeah, I'm coming." She raised her eyebrows. "Don't suppose I'll see you around, will I?"

BB shrugged. "I'm at the Mission House on Fridays. I go to church there most Sundays. Maybe I'll see you then?"

Pritt laughed. "Don't hold your breath, lover boy." She started walking down the street.

Tamara hesitated, then nodded. "Maybe. Have a good night." She hurried to catch up with Pritt.

BB sighed. "I hope I planted a seed, Lord. The rest is up to You."

* * *

Wendy pulled to the bus stop, and BB climbed into the stretch van. He smiled at her. "Thanks, Wendy. I appreciate it."

"You know we'll always come get you. What happened?" She put the vehicle in gear and headed down the street.

BB explained as she drove. Wendy listened, then asked, "Are we going back to your dorm or to get your car?"

BB hesitated. "I need to talk to you and Dad first. I want help making a decision."

Wendy glanced over at him, then back to her driving. "Okay. We'll wait until we get home. Ben will want to see you."

Ben was BB's thirteen-year-old brother. "Why is he still up? It's past ten."

"We received an emergency foster about four hours ago. Newborn. She's keeping the neighborhood awake."

That explained the worn look on Wendy's face. BB shook his head. "One of those. You've had your share of screamers these past few months." He looked out the window at the cars on the freeway. Not too much traffic tonight. Yet.

Wendy smiled tight-lipped. "Yes, we have. But they need love as much as the contented ones. Probably more so."

"They'll get it with you and Dad." BB hoped the compliment would help.

Wendy threw in, "And Ben. He has a real way of quieting the squirmiest ones."

Ben was six years BB's junior. His brother had come a long way since the days he didn't talk or communicate at all. He was now in seventh grade with his "non-neurodivergent" peers. And functioning well. All the special education, counseling, and mentoring Ben had received— and continued to receive—had made a major difference. He was learning.

Too well sometimes. BB chuckled to himself. Ben had definite opinions about the world and how it should go. But he was a loving brother to the infants Wendy and Dad fostered. Which, with today's emergency one, numbered four. Unless they'd snuck in a fifth? Hopefully not. The triplets were temporary until their mom got back on her feet and could handle three four-month-olds at the same time.

Mialma, the family's black Labrador, met the van at the driveway. Wendy and BB climbed out of the car. BB ruffled the dog's ears. "Hey, girl. How you doing?" It had been two weeks since BB had been home. He stopped walking. "Listen."

Wendy turned her head. "I don't hear anything."

BB smiled. "Neither do I. The screamer must have worn herself out."

Wendy breathed a long, slow sigh. "Finally. Maybe the neighbors will let us stay." She led the way across the wraparound porch to the back door and into the house.

Dad had an infant cradled on his shoulder, sleeping. He whispered, "Shh."

Ben walked into the kitchen with an older baby in the same position and echoed his father. "Shh."

BB whispered, "I get the picture." He shut the ringer off on his phone and laid it in the basket on the counter. All phones were to remain in silent mode once the little fosters were asleep. Firm family rule.

BB offered his arms. "Who needs the break?"

Ben held out the child in his arms. "Me. I've been walking longer." BB accepted the baby from his brother, keeping her tightly wrapped in the receiving blanket. He wondered if she had been the screamer. No, that one would be with Dad. The littlest one needed the most care, obviously.

Dad passed his charge to Wendy. Wendy took the infant and began the slow dance women do to keep babies asleep. BB had yet to learn the routine's choreography, so he rocked back and forth. After another five minutes of quiet time, Wendy motioned with her head. "I think we can try laying them down." She kept her tone just above a whisper.

BB followed his adoptive mom into the nursery. Two cribs were occupied. Two were empty. Wendy indicated one of the cribs nearest the door. "There. Put her down."

BB lay the baby in the crib, slowly removed his arms from under her body, and prayed she would stay asleep. Wendy moved beside him and placed her infant next to his. She tucked them close together, patted their tummies, then stepped back.

Silence. Other than sucking noises and grunts and baby sighs. Success. Wendy held up a hand for an "air" high five. BB grinned and returned it. They backed out of the room and closed the door. Quietly. Very quietly. And breathed out in relief.

Wendy and BB snuck into the kitchen. BB hugged his dad and then touched his knuckles with Ben. Dad kept his voice soft. "I thought you were out to dinner. What's going on?"

BB grabbed a drink from the fridge, swallowed half of it, then set it down. "I want to talk about changing schools."

Wendy's eyes narrowed. "You've only been there one semester. Why?"

"Can we sit?" BB jerked his head over his shoulder.

Wendy chuckled. "Of course. I'm sorry. Living room or den?"

"Living room." More seats. Less standing.

"That serious, hmm?" Wendy led the procession to the living room.

Ben flopped in the recliner. Dad removed him. "Find another seat, or I'll send you to bed." He grinned at Ben.

Ben flounced to his place on the couch next to BB. Wendy took the rocker. Dad sat in the recliner. He leaned forward to look at his son. "What's this about?"

BB started, "First, let me tell you what happened tonight and why I called Wendy." He detailed the invitation from his roommates for dinner, then explained the ruse with the fake ID. "That's when I decided to leave. I rode downtown with the guys, so my car is still at the dorm." BB drew in a deep breath. "I want to switch to junior college for the first two years, then transfer my last two."

Dad raised his eyebrows. "And live at home?"

"In an apartment on my own. Or with a roommate. I don't mind living with someone or living away. But I need control of the living situation."

"Control? What's going on at the dorm?"

BB slumped back on the couch. "Parties. Loud parties. Drunken parties. Smoking. And not only cigarettes." He held up his hand. "And yes, I've asked them not to, and yes, they've blown me off. Literally. Blew smoke in my face."

He never wanted to punch someone out as much as he wanted to Vic. But he hadn't. He'd remembered Whose he was and Who he served. And had held his breath and his temper.

Wendy scowled and shook her head. Dad studied the floor with a tight-lipped frown, then said, "You won't be able to control every aspect of your life, BB. That privilege belongs to the Lord. He may have put you in this room with these guys for a purpose."

BB nodded. "I've thought of that. I've prayed about it. I have, Dad. And I believe this last stunt of theirs crossed the line. Trying to get me to do something unlawful goes beyond being annoying."

Dad stared into BB's eyes for a long moment. Then he nodded. "Agreed. On principle. If you say you've prayed about it, and the Lord told you not to cross the line, there's your answer." He raised his eyebrows. "But did you ask, or did you tell the Lord where the line is?"

BB dropped his gaze. "I think I told Him. Said I'd put up with a lot of stuff but nothing against the law."

Wendy interjected, "I agree with you. You shouldn't be conned into doing something that would put you in trouble with law enforcement." Her tone sounded firm. Quiet, but firm.

Dad shrugged. "There might be a time"—he waved Wendy and BB's objections down— "where He would. But this isn't it, I agree." He leaned back in his chair. "You want to sleep here tonight?"

"With all these babies? Sure, why not? I'll probably get a better night's sleep." Better than with three drunk roommates. He got up and went to the kitchen to retrieve his phone long enough to text Leeland he wouldn't be at the dorm. Courtesy. Not that the others would care, but they agreed on the protocol per dorm regulations.

Text messages blew up his phone.

Man, can you give us a ride home?

We're at the police station.

The IDs didn't work. We got busted for underage drinking.

We need a ride.

BB, you there?

It's serious, man. We need you. We can't leave without a ride.

BB?

BB grinned.

Scripture echoed in his mind. *Do not gloat when your enemy falls.*

BB swallowed his sense of self-righteousness. He

looked at Wendy and Dad. "Um…can we help some…uh…friends? Who need a ride home from jail?"

Dad grinned. "Let me guess."

BB nodded. He couldn't keep the chuckle from his voice. "Yeah. They need someone to pick them up. Can we do that?"

Dad stood and looked at Wendy. She nodded. "I think Ben and I can hold the fort until you get back."

Ben gave out an exaggerated but quiet groan. "My arms are sore."

Dad ruffled Ben's hair. "As long as you stay very quiet, you should be fine." He pulled his shoes on, grabbed his keys, and waved BB out the door.

No sooner had the two men reached the van than an infant wail lifted into the night. Followed by a second. Then, a third. Dad shoved the keys into BB's hands and chuckled. "Drive. Let's go."

BB hesitated only a second, then jumped in the van, started the motor, and pulled out of the driveway. He looked at his dad. "You sure you want to leave Wendy?"

Dad pointed down the street. "Drunks over diapers."

BB grinned. "I hear you." He turned the van forward and drove.

* * *

SATURDAY

Dad dropped the four first-year students at the dorm. BB ensured his roommates got into the room, retrieved his car, and drove home. It was after one a.m. when he arrived at the house. He stepped out of his car and listened. No babies crying. Good, good. Dad had made it into the house without rousing the neighborhood. Could BB do the same?

He tiptoed around to the back door, entered the code for the electronic lock, and slipped into the kitchen. A single light glowed in the family room.

Dad lay on the couch, an infant on his chest. BB shook his head. He snuck over, pulled the baby off his dad, and cuddled it on his shoulder. The child didn't stir. BB walked the little one to the nursery, found the empty crib, and placed his bundle on its back. He straightened the sleeper the child wore, then slipped out the door.

BB returned to the family room, threw a cover over his dad, and then retired to his room. Yes, it remained *his* room. At least for another year. His plan, not Dad and Wendy's. He kept it to motivate him to get his act together and get out on his own. He also kept it so Ben didn't feel abandoned. Another year, and maybe his little brother would accept BB being gone permanently.

BB changed into pajamas, stretched out on his bed, and

closed his eyes. Moments later, a bump came from under the bed. BB rolled over and looked into the eyes of Mialma, the Lab. He grinned at her, patted her head, and whispered, "Hiding from the noise, huh, girl? I don't blame you. I won't tell." Mialma wagged her tail and shuffled deeper under the bedframe. BB shook his head. *Lord, they need me right now, don't they? I'm glad I'm here. Thank You for arranging this.* BB closed his eyes and slept.

* * *

Morning came early with fussy, hungry cries from the four fosters. BB rolled out of bed to join Mick, Wendy, and Ben in the nursery. Wendy pointed to the remaining infant, who had yet to be claimed. "That one's yours. His name is Chris."

BB swooped the little boy from his crib. After a quick change of clothes and diaper, the child settled into his arms to drink a bottle. BB hummed as he rocked the infant. The youngster smiled at BB, letting the formula dribble over his chin and down his too-thin cheeks. BB chuckled. "None of that, now. You need every drop you can get." He dabbed at the escaping liquid and wiggled the bottle to get his charge to eat again. After the bottle was empty, BB gently placed Chris over his shoulder and rubbed the infant's back to promote a healthy burp. Which he received in short order.

He walked with the baby into the family room. The other babies were enjoying tummy time. Well, two out of three were enjoying tummy time. There was always one who had to protest. Wendy picked up the squealer and rocked him until he settled, and she could put him down again.

Ben sat in the rocker, close enough to help but far enough away he didn't have to be the first responder. He muttered, "Aldi hates being on his stomach. He should learn to roll over."

BB moved to the floor with the children and rubbed Chris' back. He looked at Wendy and asked, "How old?"

She pointed around the room. "Sassy, Chris, and Aldi

are triplets and all four months old. May, who came in yesterday, is just over two weeks."

BB shook his head. "These poor little ones." He stared at the babies. "Will they be able to go back to their natural parents?"

Dad shook his head. "The triplets have a single mom, and she's having a hard time adjusting. Three at once was a lot. If she gets some help, she might be able to take them home."

Wendy's tone darkened. "Big if. Maybe she'll take one. But I'm not even sure about that."

BB motioned to May. "What about the emergency?

Dad's voice filled with sadness. "May won't be going anywhere soon. No family and Mom is in jail." He shook his head. "No word on who the father is. Either she doesn't know, or she's not telling out of fear. We need to be praying for her."

"What about adoption?"

"May was surrendered at the hospital. She was supposed to be an 'adopted at birth' baby, but her mom fell off the wagon. She's a crack baby. We're getting her weaned off the crack. But the parents-to-be didn't want to deal with the possible implications."

"Implications? Like what?" BB couldn't imagine what would prevent a couple from loving "their" child.

"Having to pick up meds to get the baby off the crack. Being embarrassed at the pharmacy. Having neighbors listen to an infant scream in withdrawal. The chance of complications later in life. Slow development. You name it. The fears are real."

BB reached out and patted the back of the littlest girl. He sat cross-legged on the carpet, then turned to look at his dad, who sat on the couch. "I'll go talk to my roommates. Maybe after bailing them out and taking them home, they'll be more inclined to listen to my requests. Maybe we can work it out."

Dad nodded. "I think that's an excellent idea."

Wendy asked. "And if it doesn't?"

"Then you'll have an extra set of hands for a few days."

Ben raised his hand. "I'll vote for that." He rocked back and forth.

Dad laughed. "We're not taking votes right now, bud. But when we do, we'll know your feelings." He sat forward in his recliner.

Sunlight slipped in through the heavily shaded curtains. Dad rose and pulled the shades open to let in the light. The babies would enjoy the warmth on their bodies. At least until nap time. Which, considering everyone just ate, shouldn't be long from now. Not at this age. BB climbed to his feet. "Anyone interested in breakfast?"

Ben kept his tone quiet. "I am, I am." He raised his hand to triple his agreement.

BB chuckled. "I know you are."

Ben flexed his shoulders. "I'm a growing boy. Everyone tells me that."

BB looked at his parents. "Dad? Wendy?" He struggled with calling her "mom." Wendy and Dad had been married less than six months. It was too soon to call her anything but Wendy. Maybe later. Maybe.

Dad shook his head. "I'll come fix coffee."

BB nodded. "I'll drink it. I have a feeling I'm gonna need it to face those guys."

Wendy came to her feet as well. "Don't project. It might go very well."

"I'll hope for the best."

Ben muttered, "And plan for the worst."

BB pointed at his brother. "You're learning too fast. I'll hope for the best and leave the outcome to the Lord."

Ben nodded once. "Right."

They left the babies on the floor, confident no one would escape the room for the few minutes the adults (plus Ben) would be gone. BB pulled out bacon, eggs, English muffins, cheese, and butter. A breakfast sandwich he could eat on the way to the dorm would work best. He raised his eyebrows at Wendy. "Do-it-yourself egg, cheese, and bacon muffin?"

Wendy smiled. "Oh, why not? Sounds good on the run."

BB fixed a quick bacon and egg sandwich for himself and Wendy, and bacon and eggs for Ben. He carried his meal to his room and chewed a mouthful while he dressed. Once he declared himself decent, he stuffed more of the sandwich into his mouth and walked back to the kitchen.

Wendy reappeared with Aldi on her shoulder. The little boy burbled and laughed and cooed. Dad held out his hands. "Here. I'll take him so you can eat."

Wendy shook her head. "From the sound of things, you're about to have your own. Sassy's had about enough tummy time for today. And probably tomorrow."

Dad laughed. "Yeah, she's not big on looking at the floor." He poured a cup of coffee for himself, put one in a to-go cup for BB, and strolled back to the family room.

BB sampled a swallow of the coffee. Yep. The amount of caffeine would keep him awake through today. Probably tonight, too. Dad's coffee was legendary. Micah Andres' brews had fueled many an all-nighter.

BB grabbed his phone, kissed Wendy on the head, fist-bumped Ben, and hugged his dad as he headed to the door. He patted Mialma as he left. Poor pup. All the commotion. She must be lonely for attention.

BB headed to the dorms. He parked, climbed the five flights of stairs, and let himself in as silently as he could. No telling what shape the others would be.

Leeland lay draped across his lower bunk sans clothes. An empty quart bottle of cheap whiskey lay beside his bed.

Vic lay in the same state, though he had half of his body under a blanket. A half-consumed container lay on the carpet by his lower bunk. Vodka had been his drink of choice. Or so BB assumed from the evidence.

Samuel slept, hanging precariously from the upper berth, half in, half out of his bed. The sonorous snores from all three sleepers indicated they'd be out for some time. It was a little past seven. BB slid to his desk, sat, and opened his physics book. He would take the time to study until the room came to life. Being Saturday, no one had classes. But Samuel and Vic had football practice at nine. Would they be awake? Should he wake them?

Let them learn responsibility. The world would teach them there were consequences to their actions. BB didn't have to say anything. Or do anything.

He played with the WWJD band on his wrist. A reminder of Who he belonged to. Who he'd dedicated his life to. Would Jesus let the men sleep? Or would He wake them for their assignment?

Hmm. Good question. A good one to ask, too. *Lord? What do You want me to do? Wake them up, or let them sleep?*

Scripture poured into BB's mind. Wake, sleeper. Stop your slumbering. A little sleep, a little slumber, a little folding of the hands, and so will your poverty come...

I hear You, Lord. I'll wake 'em up.

When would be the next question. He'd wait until eight and then give them the first wake-up call. A second call would depend on the reception after the first one.

At eight, BB closed his textbook and pushed back his papers. He rose to his feet and tried Samuel first. BB clasped his roommate's shoulder and shook him. "Samuel. On your feet, man. You've got practice in an hour. Time to go, man."

Samuel rolled away and muttered something unintelligible. Probably best undecipherable as well. BB moved to Vic and tried again. "Vic. Wake up. You've got football practice. You gotta get up."

Vic sat. His eyes were unfocused. "What?"

BB chuckled to himself. "Wake up, dude. You've got football practice. Coach takes spring training seriously.

You've got an hour to look alive."

"What?"

BB stepped out of swinging range. "Wake up, Vic. You need to get moving."

Vic stared at BB. Vic blinked, blinked again, then groaned. He pulled himself to his feet, grabbing the upper bunk for support. He pulled all of BB's blankets down in his effort. Vic dropped them on the floor, stepped across them, then grabbed Samuel's bunk and shook it as hard as he could. "Samuel! Out of bed." He growled at his teammate. "Get up, you lazy dog."

While "dog" wasn't the word Vic used, it was the only translation BB allowed in his head.

Rattling Samuel's bunk roused Leeland. He fell on the floor, then rolled under the bed. The confused man shouted, "Earthquake!"

Vic kicked at the cowering figure. "Get up, stupid." He half-pulled Samuel from his bunk, landing the man on his back on the floor. "Let's go. Hit the showers. We can't let Coach know we were out late. He'll put us on the practice squad."

BB stepped aside as the two men scrambled to take turns in the shower and threw on clothes. Samuel asked, "Breakfast?"

"You want to throw up all over the field? Suck it up, buttercup. We don't have time." Vic shoved Samuel out the door. BB heard them pounding down the hall.

Leeland's muffled voice came from under the bed. "Is it over?"

BB grinned. "Yes, Leeland. The earthquake's over."

Leeland crawled out from under the bed. He grabbed a blanket, covered himself, sat, and looked at BB. "Must have been a big one. My bunk rattled like crazy." He cocked his head. "Why didn't you take cover?"

BB picked up his blankets and threw them on his bed. He straightened the covers, tucked the blankets under the mattress, and placed the pillow in the center of the headboard. Everything neat. In place. He called over his shoulder, "It was only Vic trying to get Samuel out of bed."

"Vic? That's not funny, dude. I could've been hurt."

"Right." BB finished his housekeeping and turned to face his roommate.

Leeland continued to sit on the floor. He ran his hand through his hair and over his eyes. "Where'd you go last night?"

BB tried to swallow his smirk. "Which time?"

Leeland had to stop and think. From the look in his eyes, not all the squirrel cages were spinning in the same direction. "Uh…what did happen last night?"

BB leaned against the bunk and said, "You guys stayed at the club. You told me the place got raided for underage drinking. You three got arrested, along with about ten others. My dad and I picked you up after you bailed out and brought you back to the dorm." BB pointed to the bottles on the floor. "Then I would guess you three had a party to celebrate."

Leeland scratched his shoulder. "I don't remember."

"Which part?"

"The drinking. I remember getting arrested. And Vic telling us not to say anything. His dad owns a judge, and he said—"

BB jumped. "His dad, what?"

"He said he owns a judge. Said the man owes him about a million favors. Vic's dad calls them in whenever Vic gets in trouble with the law. It's how Vic got into school. His dad's friend pulled strings. That's what Vic says, anyhow."

BB filed all the information away. Verify first. Then, decide what, if anything, he should do about it. He extended his hand to Leeland and helped the man off the floor. "Maybe go shower. You might feel more human."

Leeland nodded. "Yeah. Probably right." He wandered to the bathroom, shut the door, and turned on the water.

BB shook his head. "Lord, if I'm here for a reason, let

me know what it is. I'm not sure I can make a dent in these guys. But it's up to You." He returned to his desk, laid his hands on the cold metal writing surface, and resumed his physics studies.

Half an hour later, Leeland emerged from the bathroom, wrapped in a towel. He meandered to his closet, pulled out some clothes, and dressed. The man pulled up a gray metal chair, leaned back on two legs, and stared at BB. After a few moments of silence, he asked, "What are you doing here, man?"

BB held his hands out over his schoolwork. "Physics."

"No, I mean here, here. At the dorm. We treat you like a dog." Leeland stopped, then admitted, "I treat my dog better than we treat you. Why are you still here?"

BB pushed back from the desk, narrowed his eyes, and stared at Leeland. "Do you guys want me to leave?"

Leeland snorted. "No. You're fun to kick around." He lowered his head, then admitted, "And you picked us up last night. Everyone else we called hung up on us."

BB's eyes narrowed a touch. "Whose idea was it to call me?"

Leeland shrugged. "Mine. After what we did at the club, I just knew you'd blow us off like all the others. But we were out of ideas. The cops said they'd take us home…in a cruiser. Yeah, that couldn't happen. The whole campus would know, and it would get back to Coach. Vic and Samuel would be benched. You were our only hope, Obi-wan." He grinned, then cocked his head to the side. "Why did you come?"

"You're my roommates. You were in trouble. I figured I could help."

"That's it? That's the only reason?" Leeland leaned forward, dropping the chair legs to the ground.

BB prayed, then said, "I figured it's what Jesus would do."

Leeland groaned and pushed his chair back. "You're one of those Christians, aren't you?"

"I'm a Christ-follower if that's what you mean."

"Same difference."

"No. Not even close." BB twirled his pencil in his hand. *Your words, Lord. Your Truth.*

Leeland snorted. "I suppose you're going to tell me the difference, right?"

BB shrugged. "Only if you want to hear it. Otherwise, no."

"Good. Keep it to yourself. I don't need someone preaching at me."

BB smiled. "That's fine. I don't preach." He turned back to his studying.

Leeland rose from his chair and went to his dresser. He fished around in the top drawer, pulled out a pair of socks, and carried them to his bunk. He straightened the covers on his bed, pounded his pillow, sat on his bunk, and put his socks on. Finally, he said, "Go on, then. What's the difference?"

BB went from observing Leeland sideways to facing him full-on. "Most people who say they are Christians mean they're not Jewish or Muslim or Hindu…it's something to put down on the survey forms. Not all of them, of course, but I'd bet the vast majority. They've attended church a couple of times, mainly on Christmas and Easter."

Leeland yawned and leaned back in his bunk. BB was clearly losing him. He stood. "Let's get breakfast. You think you can eat after last night's binge?"

Leeland came to his feet. "If you're buying, I'm eating."

"I'll buy. This time." There were more important issues to worry about than who paid for a meal. At least at this point. There was a strategy in BB's decision to move the conversation. Long talks in the same location would lose Leeland. By changing the scenery, Leeland would pay better attention. At least, that was BB's hope.

They went to the cafeteria. It seemed quiet. On Saturdays, the campus emptied as students found someplace else to be. The metal tables with their benches were less than half-full. Sunshine filtered through the floor-to-ceiling windows that needed cleaning. Smells of sausage, biscuits, and coffee trickled into BB's brain. The bacon-egg-and-cheese sandwich he'd had at home no longer satisfied his appetite. Something more would be better.

The two men lined up with their trays at the buffet line. BB pulled out a plate, inspected it for cleanliness, then went for eggs and potatoes. The sausage patties were overcooked and looked like hockey pucks. The links weren't much better. Bacon lay limp and undercooked. BB passed. The pancakes appeared fresh and steaming. He grabbed three cakes and five syrup packets and placed them on his tray. He finished his plate with a biscuit, went to the cashier, and smiled at the surly man. "Mine and the tray of the gentleman behind me."

Surly grunted, took BB's card, and waited for Leeland to finish loading two plates with some of everything. The cashier swiped BB's card. BB's eyes widened as he watched the points come off. Yikes. He'd need to refigure his food budget. Ah, well, he could cut back for a few days.

They got a table near the window, looking over the common grounds. An array of students dotted the yards. The nonchalance of the older class mixed with the exuberance of the younger. Stretched out on blankets or towels, they were enjoying the sunshine and each other. Neon frisbees spun through the air. Footballs intercepted the discs, and good-natured discussions followed. Saturday life at college.

Leeland shoveled his food into his mouth. BB chuckled. "There's more where that came from, you know."

"Not on my income. I'm about outta my food budget until the first of the month."

Ten days from today. BB shook his head. "How you gonna make it, man?"

"Friends. Soup kitchen. Church dinners. There's always supper for someone somewhere." Leeland scraped the eggs from his plate and mixed them with the remaining potatoes.

"So Christians are good for something, hmm?" BB sipped his coffee. Not his dad's coffee. Dad's could walk. This would barely stumble. But it was caffeine, so not to be turned down.

Leeland shrugged. He picked up the bacon, limp though it was, and fed it into his mouth. He chewed, swallowed, and then pointed with his fork. "You were telling me the difference between Christians and you."

"Christians and Christ-followers." BB lifted a prayer. "Christ-followers are people who have chosen to live by the ideal of 'what would Jesus do?' in every situation. And once you know what He would do, you do it."

"Yeah?" Leeland dredged his remaining bacon in his pancake syrup. "And regular Christians don't?"

"They may ask the question, but they're not automatically going to live by the answer. They can find reasons around it."

"Examples, man. Give me examples."

"Last night, when you called for a ride. I asked myself, 'What would Jesus do?' Giving you a lift back to the dorm seemed like the easy answer. So, I came and picked you and the others up."

Leeland finished the food on his plate. He stared at BB sideways. "How do you know what he would do?"

"We read what He said and did and follow it."

"Like?" Leeland led BB on.

"Like love your enemies. Do good to people who mistreat you. Help those around you who can't help themselves. Treat others the way you want to be treated."

Leeland mulled over the idea. "Even when they don't treat you right?"

"Especially then. We're supposed to be examples of how Jesus lived."

Leeland squinted his eyes and frowned. "Tough way to be."

"Yeah, they crucified Him for it. We don't expect to be treated much better."

"And you want others to follow you? That's ridiculous. You're supposed to be showing people the good life…all the ways they can get ahead and win. This doesn't sound like much fun."

"Jesus didn't promise it would be fun. Only that it would be worth it."

Two young women walked by the table. One blonde, one redhead. The redhead smiled at BB. She cocked her head and tossed her ponytail. "Hey, BB. We've got a sorority party on Friday afternoon. It's going to be wild. You want to join us?"

BB shook his head. "No, I've got a late class. I'll pass."

The young woman, Riley, raised her eyebrows. "You sure? We'll probably run late. Much later than your class. It will be fun, I promise. You'll get to meet all the important people on campus. My parties are legendary."

Leeland held up his hand. "I'll come."

The blonde woman snorted and shook her head. "You're not invited, Leeland." Her voice cut the air. "This is for the cream only." She glared at Leeland. Leeland ignored her.

BB shook his head again. "No, Riley. I'm not a party person. I'll pass."

She touched his cheek. "You could be. We could make you one. I've got women who would love to make your acquaintance. You'd be a great escort." She smiled. "Consider yourself chosen."

"No." He made his voice as firm as he could be without being rude. "Thanks anyhow."

Riley sniffed. "You miss this party, and you might not get another chance. Think it over. Carefully. Very carefully." The two women walked off.

Leeland chuckled. "You don't know what you're missing. Those two throw all the best parties on campus.

You attend one, and you're good for life. Turn them down, and you could have an enemy you don't want."

BB shrugged. "I'll take that chance."

The cafeteria doors slammed open. Burly, buff young men spilled into the room, all trying to be first through the entrance. Yells and curses bounced off the quiet, ending the peace. Football practice must be over.

Samuel and Vic scrambled to BB's table. Vic mocked, "Hey, losers. What are you doing?" He glared at Leeland. "You bought breakfast? You said you didn't have any money. You owe me."

Leeland poked a fork at BB. "I don't have any money. BB paid for breakfast."

"Yeah?" Vic stared at BB. "You buying, huh?"

BB prayed. "I paid for Leeland."

Vic taunted, "Then you won't mind paying for us, right?"

BB felt the nudge. "No, I don't mind this time."

Vic yelled around the room, "Hey! BB's buying. Get in line, boys."

Leeland's eyes widened. His jaw dropped open. Even Samuel objected. "Not cool, Vic."

But the stampede had started. Free food is free food and not to be questioned. BB waved Leeland off. He held Vic's eyes. "This time. Go for it."

Vic walked to the line and dug his elbow into one of his teammate's ribs. The jostling and joshing continued until the trays were heavy-laden with food.

BB looked at Samuel. "Go ahead. I said I would."

Samuel shook his head. "Not like that. I'll pay for my own." He strode to the serving line.

Leeland lowered his head. "That Vic. He's so full of himself. Someone needs to take him down a peg."

BB shrugged. "Someone will. His kind usually meets a bad end."

Leeland looked up and around the room at the players

taking full advantage of BB's "generosity." "What does your Jesus say about this?"

BB smiled. "'If your enemy is hungry, feed him. If he's thirsty, give him something to drink.' Jesus commands me to love people the way He loves me. Jesus loves Vic. Maybe not what he does, but He loves his soul." BB snorted slightly. "And he does have one."

Leeland muttered, "I'm not convinced."

BB grinned.

Vic and Samuel returned to the table. Vic's tray was loaded with three plates of all he could get. Samuel had only what he could afford. Which remained far less than what Vic took.

Vic noticed. He crammed an egg into his mouth, then asked, "Why aren't you eating?"

"I'm eating what I can pay for."

Vic scoffed. "Ah, BB doesn't care, do you, now? You scholarship types are usually rolling in the dough. Tell me I'm lying."

BB chose his words carefully so he wouldn't be. "Most scholarship students I know who aren't on a sports team are careful what they spend. Their tuition covers classes and books but not living expenses."

Vic speared his fork into a sausage patty. "They're losers. You want things paid for, you have to be on a team. Sports is where the money is."

BB let the subject drop. Leeland studied him. Probably wanted to know what Jesus would do about Vic. Leave Leeland in his ignorance. Best thing BB could do at this point.

BB finished his coffee and stood. Between mouthfuls, Vic suggested, "Everyone needs an alibi for Friday night. Field house got broken into. That's why Coach broke us loose early."

BB cocked his head. "Why would we need alibis? They're not going to question the entire student body."

Vic shrugged. "You never know. I heard they found a dead body inside. They might look wider than you think."

BB asked, "Any idea who it might be? Student? Faculty? Vagrant?"

"Someone in our dorm, I think." Vic chewed his toast. "Maybe on our floor."

Leeland's eyes went wide. "Who?"

Vic shook his head. "Don't know. Just telling you what I heard. We'll probably know more later. But get your alibis straight."

Leeland sank back in his chair. "I was with you guys."

Samuel's eyes narrowed. "Were you? I don't remember."

Leeland banged his fist on the table. "I was. We went to our room. Vic got drunk on vodka. I finished a bottle of Red Mike's, and you toked your way to unconsciousness."

Vic smirked. "You know that for a fact? Who stayed awake the longest?"

Leeland lowered his head to his fists on the table. "I don't remember."

Samuel laughed. "Joking, man. You're safe."

Vic eyed BB. "You're not. We don't know where you were last night."

BB shrugged it off. "Leeland has the text that I stayed with the folks. Four fosters will vouch for my whereabouts." *All underage, but Vic doesn't need to know that.*

"Who says you didn't pay them?"

BB didn't rise to the bait. "That will be for the police to decide, I guess." He nodded to Leeland. "I'll see you later. I'm going back to the room to finish studying."

BB walked away from the table. He heard Vic laughing. "He's so easy."

Lord, only Your Spirit in me is going to handle him. Left to myself, I'd deck him. Keep me in check. Please. Don't let me dishonor You. He walked away.

* * *

MONDAY

Ben slid his lunch tray onto the table and climbed onto the bench to eat. The junior high school cafeteria filled up for the second lunch. Eighth graders got to eat first. Then, the seventh graders. Ben picked a table where he could be by himself. He liked being alone. He usually ended up that way anyhow. He may as well like it.

He laid his sketch pad and pencils beside his tray. The pencils went in order, tallest to smallest. Then the eraser. The brush. He would sketch Tricia today. Ben liked her. She talked with him. She was nice to him. He would draw her picture.

He cut his meat patty into four quarters. Ben arranged them to sit neatly on his plate. One at twelve, one at three, one at six, and one at nine o'clock. He picked up the twelve o'clock segment and bit into it. He chewed precisely ten times, then swallowed. He took one level forkful of peas, placed it in his mouth, and chewed. Ten times. Swallow. One fork of mashed potatoes. Chew.

The nine o'clock quarter followed. Then peas. Potatoes. Chew.

Six o'clock. Then three o'clock. Make sure there are enough peas for the final bite. Everything had to come out even.

Ben finished his meal, pushed his tray aside, and pulled up a blank page in his sketch pad. He began drawing from memory. Tricia's hair. Auburn. Wavy. Pulled to the side and held back with a ribbon. A long, pale blue ribbon. It would be light strokes. Ben only drew in charcoal. He liked charcoal. His first drawings were with a stick in the dirt. Then he got a pencil. With a pencil, he could make things look the way he liked. It felt safe.

He shaded and outlined her eyes. Light gray with green flecks. Ben noticed these things. Noticed the way her smile turned up on one side more than the other. Noticed the way he could barely see her top teeth. He drew her without her braces. Beautiful and kind and peaceful.

A body jarred his arm. Ben kept the pencil from marring the portrait. "Watch it."

A voice sneered, "Who you talking to, weirdo?"

Craig Wilson. Ben's chief tormentor. Ben ground his teeth. *Jesus, help me not answer back.* Ben moved the picture away from the edge of the table.

Craig snatched it from him. "What's this? A love letter?" He held it in the air. "Oh, look! He's coloring pictures. Who's this supposed to be?" He showed the picture to the three boys with him. They all laughed. Of course, they did. They laughed at everything Craig did.

Ben tried to grab the portrait back from Craig, but the taller boy held it high. "I know who this is! This is supposed to be Tricia." He yelled, "Tricia! Your lover boy is drawing pictures of you."

Ben saw the lunch monitor, Mr. Guthrie, coming across the room in a hurry. Ben rose to grasp his work, only to have Craig come down with the full force of his elbow connecting with Ben's eye socket. Craig crumpled up the portrait and dropped it on the table. He pretended to swing at Ben.

Mr. Guthrie stepped between the boys. He demanded, "What's going on here?"

Ben stayed silent. He pulled the picture to himself and

smoothed it out. The lines were ruined. He scrunched it back up. He would draw another one.

Craig pointed at Ben and sneered. "He hit my elbow."

The monitor snorted. "With his eye, of course."

"He planned it that way. He wants it to look like I hit him. I didn't."

Mr. Guthrie looked at Ben's eye. "Are you seeing okay?"

Ben nodded. "Yes." Give them nothing more.

"Did this happen by accident?" Mr. Guthrie's eyes narrowed.

Ben tossed his ruined portrait on his tray. "Yes."

Mr. Guthrie glared at Craig. "I've got my eye on you. No more 'accidents.' You're one incident away from expulsion."

Craig shrugged. "I don't care. I can do without this school. I play baseball. I'm going to be in the big leagues."

"You've got a few years to get there. Teams aren't fond of dropouts. Makes them nervous. What else would you quit, hmm? Think about it."

Craig grunted, gathered his followers, and left.

Mr. Guthrie picked up the wadded paper and opened it. His eyes grew wide. "Ben, this is amazing."

"No, it's not. It's all ruined." Ben lowered his head.

"It is now, but it was fantastic. It looks exactly like Tricia. I would recognize that smile anywhere." He cocked his head. "But where are her braces?"

"I don't see her with them when I look at her."

Mr. Guthrie nodded. "I can tell. You did this during lunch?"

"Yes, sir."

"Are you taking art classes?"

Ben looked up at the teacher. "Do I need permission to draw at lunch?"

"Of course not. No, not at all. I think you should show this to Ms. Wellford. She would love to see your work."

Ben lowered his head again. "I only draw in charcoal."

"Then it's time you learned some different techniques. Come on. We're going to surprise a friend."

Ben rose to his feet. He picked up his sketch pad and followed Mr. Guthrie from the cafeteria. What trouble had he caused now?

* * *

BB walked from his Monday morning class back to the dorm. As he approached, he saw an unfamiliar man coming out of his room, arms laden with a bundle. BB yelled, "Hey! What are you doing?"

The stranger looked at BB, turned, and fled down the dimly lit corridor. BB shot off in hot pursuit. He'd almost reached the fleeing man when the suspect dropped what he carried. Papers and books scattered across the floor. BB hesitated. Give chase, or gather up what had been stolen?

BB stopped and began scooping up the looseleaf pages, the composition folder, and the heavy textbook. Turning the materials over, he realized he retrieved his own physics books. The thief had stolen his homework.

BB glared at the figure as it disappeared around the corner. He returned to his room and checked for any signs of a break-in. Nothing. The doorframe looked pristine.

A head stuck out of the room next to BB's. "I heard a shout. Everything okay?" Grady, a groggy-eyed freshman, looked over from his neighboring room.

BB nodded. "Yeah, someone broke in." He looked at the door and muttered, "Or was let in." He turned back to Grady. "You got any Scotch tape?"

"Sure. What for?"

"Fingerprints."

Grady disappeared into his room and came out with a roll of cellophane tape. He handed it to BB.

"Thanks." BB tore off thin strips and covered the individual keys. He delicately rubbed the button and then placed the tape on a clean sheet of notebook paper.

Grady nodded. "Cool. Where'd you learn that?"

"My Popdad." BB corrected himself. "Granddad."

"He a cop?"

"Something like that." BB did not explain. How do you explain, "The Office"? Grady cocked his head and looked at BB but didn't ask.

BB handed the tape back to him. "Thanks. I appreciate it."

"I hope it works."

"I'll let you know."

Grady disappeared back into his room and shut the door. BB went into his room to check if anything else had been disturbed.

Leeland's towel still hung over his bunk. Vic's clothes were strewn across the floor, as always. Books, cords, and notecards were mixed in piles on the desks of the other three men as always. Everything had been left the same as when BB left the room. Laptops were still on desks, and monitors and electronics all still in place. The thief had targeted BB. Why?

No harm, no foul. Except someone had access to the room who shouldn't have. Which meant…

BB texted his roommates, only to see them coming around the corner. He set his phone down. "Glad you guys are here. Someone came out of the room when I came up the hall."

Samuel's head jerked. "Out of our room?"

"Yeah. He's got our keycard. Only way he can have access."

Vic shrugged. "Maybe. Maybe he got lucky figuring the code."

Samuel shook his head. "Naw, he'd have to have the card for the code to work." His eyes narrowed. "Did you get a look at him?"

"From the back. Big guy. Tall. Heavy. Blond hair. Chased him down the hall. He dropped what he'd stolen, though."

Leeland looked around the room. "Doesn't look like he got anything important."

Samuel nodded. "What did he have?"

"My physics book and homework." BB leaned against the top bunk.

Leeland turned to look sideways at BB. "Your homework? Who steals homework?"

Vic popped a gummy in his mouth. "A loser." He turned away and dropped his locker bag on the floor.

BB shrugged. "I want to get the new keycards and change the code."

Samuel nodded. "Agreed." He reached into his wallet and pulled out the blank card.

Leeland reached for his wallet but came up empty. He stared at the floor, then looked at Vic. "I gave you my wallet last night. I was too drunk to be trusted."

Vic snorted, "You're always too drunk." He did not produce the wallet, however. He moved to his dresser and dumped his belongings from his field bag.

Leeland held out his hand. "Give it to me."

Vic shook his head. "I don't think we need new cards. Whoever broke in didn't get anything important. BB scared him off. He won't be back." He resumed putting away his gear.

Samuel stepped over to his teammate. He towered over him. "Give it up, Vic. I want new cards. You may not care, but I have some serious equipment they could steal. The dorm manager is only here until two. We can get them now and be done with it."

Vic glared at his friend. "I said no."

Samuel shrugged. He looked at BB. "Then they both get locked out. I'm going."

Odd for Samuel to buck Vic. But maybe he'd tired of the games. BB nodded and moved to the door. Leeland demanded, "Give me my wallet, Vic."

Vic pulled it out from his drawer and tossed it to Leeland. "Fine. Have it your way. Waste of time." He stuck his own wallet in his back pocket and joined the others at the door.

The four men walked down the corridor. BB carried his books as evidence. Mostly, he wanted to protect the sheet with the fingerprints. But he needed to keep it from getting messed up, so he carried it inside the books.

Leeland searched his wallet, then looked up in dismay. "I can't find my card. It's not in here." He looked at BB. "I know I had it last night. I checked to see if it worked. It's been acting up."

BB nodded. "I remember. We had to have it reset last week."

Samuel frowned. "Well, we know whose card they have." He glared at Leeland.

"And how they got it." Vic snorted. "Who else do you owe money to?"

Leeland protested, "No one. I didn't give my card to anyone. You had the wallet last night. I gave it to you as we left."

Confrontation was coming. Could BB stop it? Should he?

Vic's eyes narrowed, and his voice became hard. "Are you accusing me of stealing from your wallet?"

Leeland drew himself up. "You had the wallet. The card was in there. Now, it's not. You connect the dots." Leeland straightened his shoulders and stood straight.

Vic swung hard and fast, knocking Leeland against the cinderblock wall. He followed the shove with a blow to the gut. Leeland doubled over in agony.

Samuel grabbed his teammate and pushed him to the side. "Knock it off! Fighting gets you kicked off the team."

Vic snarled, "He called me a thief."

BB stayed out of the fray. He felt as Leeland did, but he wouldn't exacerbate the situation by mouthing off. He helped Leeland straighten up.

Vic pointed at Leeland. "You better remember who owns you."

Samuel pulled Vic's arm. "Let's go. We'll get the cards and fight later." Samuel led the group down the corridor to the elevators and down to the dorm manager's office.

The manager, Mr. Peterson, crossed his arms and leaned against an oak desk. He seemed less than impressed with the story of the break-in. But the missing card caught his attention. "Cost you $25 to replace the lost card. We don't like replacing those because someone was too careless to take care of them. Next time, it's $50."

Leeland objected, "But I didn't lose it. It was—"

BB pulled out his wallet and handed his credit card to Mr. Peterson. "Here. Put it on my account. I'll cover his. There's some question about how the card might have been lost."

He waited until all four roommates had new cards. Mr. Peterson instructed them, "You each have a new code to get in. No one else's code will work for your card. More secure that way. And we can find out who opened the door last."

BB stuck out his bottom lip. "Impressive. And interesting. This will settle some disputes, anyhow."

Peterson drawled, "That's the idea." He settled back in his chair and looked at the calendar on the wall. Days were crossed off. "VACATION" scrawled in giant letters across April. Something to look forward to? BB could only guess.

BB pulled out the sheet with the tape. "I took these fingerprints off the door. Once the police eliminate ours, they can find who broke in."

BB saw Vic's eyes flare, then narrow. Vic asked sharply, "When did you do that?"

Samuel laughed. "I want to know where you learned that trick?" He took the paper and examined the prints. "Cool."

"My granddad taught me. Don't ask. I never did."

Samuel glanced at BB for a moment, then chuckled.

Mr. Peterson took the sheet. "I'm not sure the police will be all that interested in who's stealing textbooks. But I'll give it to them."

BB nodded. "I appreciate it. I think this might have been personal. I'd like to know who wanted to steal my stuff." Bluffing. He bluffed. He wouldn't know the thief anyhow.

Vic shrugged. "Like every student has fingerprints on file." He gazed at his fingernails. Almost too nonchalant.

"No, but anyone who's been in trouble before likely has."

Vic scoffed. "The police don't care enough—"

BB smiled a straight-lipped smile. "My granddad still has connections." Vic jerked and stared hard at BB. BB filed the actions away for further consideration.

Vic snarled, "It wouldn't be legal."

"It'd be calling in a favor." BB kept from sneering at Vic. Barely.

Samuel shoved Vic. "Like you're always doing. And saying your dad does. I want to know who broke into our room." He eyed Mr. Peterson. "Do we need to file charges or something?"

Vic shoved Samuel out of his way. "I'm not wasting time on this. I got better things to do. Suit yourselves." He pointed at Leeland. "Remember what I said." He turned on his heel and walked out of the office.

Leeland slumped against the wall. "He's right."

BB shook his head. "No one can own someone else. Pay him back what you owe him, then don't borrow more."

Leeland sniffed. "Easy for you to say. He keeps adding interest."

Samuel grumbled, "Yeah, he's bad about that. Regular loan shark. Once he gets his hooks in you, it's tough to get free."

BB eyed Samuel. "You owe him money, too?" How many people were indebted to Vic?

Samuel shook his head. "Took me months to get the debt paid off. He needs me to watch his back, so he let me off easy. But I know some others who are into him deep."

Mr. Peterson cleared his throat. "If you don't want me to get involved in this, I suggest you take it out of my office."

The three men walked out into the foyer. The aroma of coffee escaped the cafeteria. It competed with the smell of wet socks. Lovely. BB focused on the coffee.

Vic hung at the corner, waiting. Samuel and Leeland fell into formation around Vic. BB trailed behind. They reached the elevator. BB punched in the floor number for the room. "I've still got studying to do." He sniffed. "Now that I have my homework."

Leeland leaned his hand against the wall. "What would you do if you hadn't got your books back?"

"Start over. Get a new book. Pretty sure the bookstore would have a used one I could buy."

Vic eyed him. "You wouldn't go looking for the guy who stole it?" Disbelief colored his expression.

"Not my job. I'd let the police handle it. But I think they've got bigger worries right now."

"Like what?"

BB's jaw fell open. "You said they found a dead body in the field house. You think they might be more interested in that?" Had Vic forgotten the rumor he so gleefully echoed Saturday?

Vic shrugged. "I heard it was nothing. Some lovesick guy got jilted and couldn't handle the loss. He killed himself."

BB's heart dropped. "That's horrible. Do you know who it might have been?"

"Didn't concern me. Don't care."

"But you said it was someone in our dorm. That means we might know him. Is his family—"

"—look, I don't know, and I don't care. Guy obviously must have been a loser. Rumor has it he left a note. Case closed. Move on." He stepped into the elevator and punched the button for the lobby.

BB grimaced. The faces of Leeland and Samuel expressed more compassion and heart. But neither added to nor detracted from Vic's opinion. Cold.

Vic, Samuel, and Leeland disembarked at the bottom floor, and BB rode back up alone. He walked to his room and tried his new keycard. It worked as advertised. BB went inside and dropped into his study chair. He placed his books back where they belonged, neat and in order. He stared at his monitor. And stared. And stared…

An idea crossed his mind. The rumor went computers were always spying on you. A camera would record all actions, even when it wasn't in use. So what if…

He'd need an expert. BB grabbed his phone and texted Addison Vaughn. Addison was the youngest of the Vaughn brothers, who were best friends to his dad, and self-appointed uncles to BB and Ben. Addison was only four years older than BB, more like a big brother. The relationships were muddled. Brothers in the Lord worked.

He texted, Need tech help. How can I replay a camera recording that isn't?

BB turned to his homework. Addison would answer when he had time. Either he would tell BB how or would find the answer for him. In a language BB could understand.

Half an hour later, a text came through with a series of instructions. BB followed them. A dozen commands later, BB had a photograph of the intruder. Full-face staring right into the camera. BB didn't recognize the man. Probably a student. The build said sports jock. Probably one of Vic's teammates. Which was why he'd reacted to the fingerprint capture. Chances were good the man's prints were on file with the police somewhere.

Was it worth pursuing? Even if Vic had set the whole stunt up, what would be accomplished by finding the thief? Would Vic suddenly see the error of his ways, come clean, and have a change of heart? Doubtful. Would it scare him into changing? Also doubtful. BB bowed his head. "Lord, I don't know if chasing this down means anything or if I should let it go. Vic thinks he's gotten away with another stunt. He thinks he's untouchable. This isn't going to change his mind or his heart. It will implicate Leeland, even though I don't think he had anything to do with it. Show me what to do."

BB sat back in his chair and waited for inspiration. Conviction. Enlightenment. An answer of some kind, anyhow.

None came. Was God saying, "You choose?" It was up to BB.

The man sighed. "Fine. I'll let it go." He turned to his studying.

But what if there had been others who suffered the same situation? If BB had the proof of who had been in his room, shouldn't he…

He stood up. "I'm going, I'm going." He would take the picture to Mr. Peterson. He'd have the fingerprints and the photo. What Mr. Peterson decided to do with it would be up to the dorm manager. BB would have reported it, and that was all that mattered.

BB grabbed an envelope from his desk and addressed it to Mr. Peterson. The man would be gone before BB arrived, but he could leave it in the inbox…or slide it under the door. Either way, he'd get it in the morning. And BB's conscience would be clear.

He picked up his books and laptop, made sure his door closed and locked, then headed downstairs to the Dorm Manager's office. He slid the envelope under the door rather than leaving it in the inbox. Somehow, it felt safer that way. More likely to be received. BB looked at his phone. He had time to get a cup of coffee and then go to his next class. First-year English. He sighed. Not his favorite subject. Bored, bored, bored. He would have tested out, but he'd already tested out of science and math. His dad insisted he take at least one "designated first-year class" for the experience. Maybe he could help someone through it. Maybe someone could help him through it. Maybe.

* * *

TUESDAY

Did he respond?
No. Can't have that. Looks bad if people can refuse me.
What are you going to do?
This is what you are going to do. Do not fail me.

Ben sat in art class. He stared at the globs of acrylic paint on his tray. Red. Yellow. Blue. Black. White. Brown. He touched the tip of a paintbrush into the red and dragged it across the sheet of paper, leaving a trail of blood. He shuddered. Not what he wanted.

Mrs. Wellford stood beside Ben. "Now try the yellow. Stronger this time."

Ben went to clean his brush. Mrs. Wellford interrupted him. "No, don't wash it off. Drag the red through the yellow. See what colors it creates."

Ben muttered, "It will make a mess." He hated messes.

Mrs. Wellford smiled. "It will make beautiful colors, Ben. Try it."

"It will ruin the yellow." Ben shuddered.

"It will enhance it. It will change it, but it won't ruin it."

Ben stared at the colors. He locked his teeth and forced his hand to desecrate the pure yellow with the red.

Orange exploded in the center. Ben stared in awe. He pulled the color from the blob, letting it trickle down the white of the page. He barely touched it to the red line and watched it darken. The blood disappeared into a burnt sunset hue.

Mrs. Wellford patted his shoulder. "Good job. Now wipe your brush then try mixing the yellow and the blue."

A tip of yellow. The lightest touch of blue.

The green of grass stared at him.

Ben looked wide-eyed at Mrs. Wellford. "It makes color."

She nodded and moved away from his desk. "Experiment." She stopped. "Have fun with it."

The teacher walked to the front of the class. "Create. Dream. Colors make our world. Let them make yours."

Ben pulled rivulets of colors and hues over the page, crisscrossing and creating ever-new hues. He stopped and examined Mrs. Wellford's hair. Could he duplicate the shades? He knew what he would do with his pencils. Could he create in color?

He dared to swirl the brown and the yellow. Not right. Not quite. Something else. Ben narrowed his eyes. He focused. Then he closed his eyes. He touched the brush in the white. He layered it on top of the brown and yellow.

Ben opened his eyes and looked at the page. Mrs. Wellford's hair color lay on the page. Not perfect. Nothing Ben did could be called perfect. People said it was, but he knew better. This wasn't right. It came close.

But not close enough. Ben crumpled the sheet and threw it in the trash. He pulled out a second sheet of paper and began again. More yellow. More white. Less brown.

He struggled. He turned the paper upside down. He squinted. He cocked his head to the side. Different light, different shadows, made the teacher's hair color change. He could catch the exact color for only a moment until she turned her head. Then, the color changed. He would have to paint the teacher in a single moment in time. He breathed deep.

He heard Dad's voice. You can do this, Ben. You can do anything. You and Jesus. Ask Him for help. Then, do what you can.

Ben muttered, "Jesus, I need help. Make these colors come out right. Please." He hesitated, then added, "If You want to. Dad says to remember that part. If You want to. Thank You."

He began again.

* * *

BB grumbled as he walked to class. Dad insisted BB could help others. He said Jesus lived to serve. BB should be thinking of how to help those in need. Even if it had to be in his dorm room. Or in English.

He muttered, "I'm sorry, Lord. I'll get my act together. I'm a Knight of the Octagon. I live to serve like You did."

He walked across the commons. The air felt damp. Spring rain made the grass glisten like diamonds. It also made his feet wet. Great. Soggy tennis shoes. The water squished between his toes. Fantastic. Oh, well, they'd dry.

He reached the auditorium where the class gathered. BB noticed a new person sitting in the front row. A female. Interesting. Transfer student? Maybe. BB took his regular seat, which happened to be beside the young woman. Not because he cared. Which he did, but let's not be obvious. Much.

Vic had also noticed the new person and was harassing her. He sat directly behind her and muttered suggestive and insulting innuendos loud enough for BB to hear. The cringe on the young woman's face moved BB to action. He stood and barked, "Vic, leave her alone."

Shocked faces turned to look at him. The professor raised his head to stare at BB. "Excuse me, Mr. Andres. Did you have something to say to the class?"

"Yes, Doctor Bush. I was telling Mr. Shields he should leave the new student alone. He's bothering her."

Dr. Bush raised an eyebrow. "Ms. Williams, is this

true?"

Ms. Williams gazed at BB, then at the professor. "Yes, sir. I was about to tell him so myself, but Mr. Andres?"—she questioned him with her glance—"spoke first."

Dr. Bush eyed Vic. "Mr. Shields, move your seat no closer than a three-row circumference from Ms. Williams. If you don't know what that means, I suggest you enroll in first-year algebra."

Vic glared at BB but then narrowed his eyes at Dr. Bush. He got up and did as he was told, however. His shoulders slumped. His feet dragged. But his eyes spoke defiance. And retribution to come.

Ms. Williams mouthed "Thank you" to BB.

Dr. Bush stood. "Now, if there are no more interruptions, we will begin. Everyone take out your syllabus. It's been brought to my attention that there was an error in one of the postings. Your midterm will actually be a week earlier."

A collective groan filled the air. BB pulled out the necessary papers. He listened as the professor updated the required information. Papers would be due a week earlier as well.

Not a problem for BB. But the looks on his classmates' faces and the whispers in the air told him not everyone had started their work. Ah, yes. Procrastinators unite. Dad, being a tax consultant, had instilled in BB the work ethic to get things done on time, if not early. April 15th tax deadlines waited for no man. Dad's lessons in punctuality served BB well in school. It would serve him well in life. *Thanks, Dad.*

The class turned to the rest of the regularly scheduled activities. BB buckled down to pay attention and learn what he needed. Once the class ended, he gathered his books and headed for the door.

Vic intercepted him with a few choice words BB decided to ignore. Vic left the room with his followers. The man never traveled alone.

Ms. Williams caught up to BB in the hall. "Thank you for speaking up in there."

BB shrugged. "I thought I'd lend a hand." He stopped, then added, "Not that I doubted you could handle it yourself."

She smiled. "I could. But I appreciate the help. I'm Julie Williams." She stuck out her hand.

"BB Andres." His backbone straightened. Just a little. For once.

"What's the BB stand for?" The woman's eyes sparkled in the hall light.

BB grinned. "It's complicated. I've got physics lab right now." He gazed at the young woman. Dark brown hair with eyes to match. Fair complected and a smile that radiated confidence. He hesitated, then offered, "How about meeting for dinner tonight? School cafeteria? About six?"

"Is this a date, Mr. Andres?"

He smiled. "No. It's a 'pre-date' date. A 'let's get to know each other first' meeting."

"I'd like that. Six, you say?"

"Right. I'm done with my classes at five. I have a Wednesday night commitment, but that's my only evening." *I'm free the rest of the time, in case this goes well.*

"Sounds good. I'll see you at the cafeteria at six." She smiled at him.

BB's chest swelled. He smiled back, turned, and practically ran to his next class. He'd met a girl. Who wanted to have dinner with him? Maybe he should offer to take her off-campus to someplace more private…

Alarm bells went off in his head. He didn't know her. Didn't know her background. Didn't know her heart. Didn't know if he should even be thinking of dating her. *Take it one step at a time.* A dinner to get to know each other. Start there. Then think about down the road.

BB found his place in the physics lab and began his work. He forced himself to stay on task. Not good to blow up the building because your mind is on other things. Like a woman.

He finished his classes at five and went back to his room. He showered, dressed, and made sure he looked presentable.

Why did he feel so smitten? He'd dated girls before. But maybe that was it. They'd been girls. This was a woman. Something totally out of his league.

BB felt the let-down overtake him. Maybe he should not show up rather than embarrass himself. But it would be rude. He would have to at least meet with her. She would ask him about himself. He would tell her the boring details of his life and that would be the end of the relationship. Get used to it.

He walked across the commons to the cafeteria. Six p.m. wasn't the busiest time to have dinner. The space would be lightly used, as most students preferred to go off-campus for fast food. But the cooks at the school cafeteria did a passable job. Better than BB would on his own. Though he did make a mean pork chop.

Julie sat near the middle of the room, a coffee cup in her hand. Maybe they had one thing in common. If it was coffee she drank and not tea.

BB approached her with his best smile. "Good evening." There were no good pick-up lines. Only "Good evening." Ah, well. Maybe being himself would work. It was all he had to offer, anyhow.

He pointed to the serving line. "Would you like dinner?"

Julie nodded. "I never turn down food."

BB grinned. So, they did have something in common. He waved his hand to allow her to proceed to the hotline. She picked up some pasta and a side salad. BB went for the ham and potatoes with a side of green beans. Less likely to stick in his teeth than the broccoli. He paid for the meals on his student card. No flashing wealth. The two students carried their trays back to where Julie left her coffee.

Julie dipped her head in what BB guessed might have been a silent prayer. Good, good. Score another agreement. Hopefully. BB followed her example and added his prayers for the food and the evening.

They ate in silence for the first couple of minutes, then BB asked, "You're a transfer student?"

Julie nodded. She swallowed the lasagna. "I came over from the junior college. My folks were late in getting all the paperwork done for admission. Once it was approved, I could start. Nothing exciting."

BB chewed the ham, swallowed, and asked, "What's your major?"

"Humanities."

"Interesting subject."

"It can be. Hard to find work, though." She smiled. "Which is why I'll work outside my field for a few years." Julie dropped her head to concentrate on her food.

BB grinned. "Understood. But worth it if you enjoy it."

The opening existed for her to ask him about his major, but she didn't. She did ask, "What do you know about the jerk who bothered me?"

"He's Vic Shields. My roommate. Along with two others." He shrugged. "Life in a dorm is interesting. You don't get to pick who you bunk with."

Julie nodded. "I don't think I would like it. I want to choose my roommate. We're going to be spending the whole year together. We should at least like each other."

"It would make it easier, true." He shifted in his seat.

"So, do you like him?" Julie chewed her lasagna between questions.

BB considered his words carefully. "He can be difficult. But I try to keep the peace as much as it depends on me." *I try.*

"What about the other guys?" She stopped, then looked at him pointedly. "You are rooming with all guys, right?" Her eyes held more than a hint of challenge.

"Yes. The dorm may be co-ed, but our room is strictly guys. Vic and Samuel are on the football team, and that's one of the coach's strictest rules. No co-ed rooms." *Thank You, Lord.*

"A little old-fashioned, isn't it?" BB sensed the disapproval in her tone.

"He thinks it keeps the guys more focused on the game. Less drama." Though, with Vic, there was always drama to be had.

BB turned the conversation to other areas of interest. "Do your parents live in this area? Do you commute, or are you full-time here?"

"My folks live in Vegas. Outside of it, anyhow. I'm full-time here. I've got a single room for now until the fall semester. Then, I'll probably get a roommate. We'll see."

Again, she asked no reciprocal question about his parents or where he lived. This wasn't going the way he had seen it in his head. Yeah, well.

"What do you do when you're not studying?" Throw the net wider.

"Oh, I don't study." She smiled. "I have a genius IQ, so I retain everything. That's how I got through high school. Listening. And out-reading the teacher."

"You must have aced all the classes." *It would be amazing to have that ability.*

"Not really. I've got about a C+ average. Good enough to get me in. That's all I cared about. I'll make certain I pass these courses, but I'm not putting any extra effort into it."

BB kept his thoughts to himself. "So, what do you do when you're not 'not' studying?" He smiled to see if she would get the joke.

Julie laughed. "I read. And I write poetry. I stay to myself, mostly."

BB nodded. "I can see how your field would appreciate that. What do you write about?"

"My feelings, mostly."

Why am I not surprised? BB nodded. "Gotcha. Have you been writing long?"

"All my life." She swallowed some of the now-cold coffee, then grinned at him. "You're not going to give up, are you?"

Three students walked past. One dropped their books. They jostled the table yet said nothing as they gathered their papers and continued on through the cafeteria.

BB asked, "Give up how?"

"Trying to find something we have in common. Or some interest we can share. I admire your persistence." Julie's eyes sparkled, and the corners of her mouth turned up.

BB eyed her. He cut more ham and chewed it before asking, "Is this a test?"

"Of course. I wanted to see how you would react to the selfish, self-centered college student. You didn't walk away, and you didn't insult me." She smiled with her eyes. "And you didn't fill the spaces with lame pick-up lines. I appreciate all of that."

Julie finished her salad and then looked BB in the eyes. "I study Marine Biology. I want to live and work on the ocean one day. And yes, there are jobs in Marine Biology." She dipped her head to the side. "I'm not a genius. And I'm not a transfer student. I switched English classes because of my labs. My parents live across town. When I'm not studying, I like to play soccer, watch football, and meet with friends. Of which I'm sorely lacking right now." She grinned, and her eyes crinkled. "Now, Mr. Andres, what are you studying? Where are you from, and what do you do for fun?"

BB relaxed. He pushed his tray to the side. "I'm studying Physics. I don't know what I want to do with it when I'm done. My…folks, I guess you would call them, live on the west end of town. We're close. I spend a lot of time with them. They foster little ones. Right now, they have four. They need all the help I can give them. I also volunteer at the Mission House. Well, a group of us volunteer there on some weekdays and every Friday." He stopped, then admitted, "This is as free as I get between classes." There remained one hill to climb. The most important one, but the one he preferred to leave for last. "On Sundays, we attend church."

"As a family?" Julie ducked as a football soared across the room.

Someone belatedly yelled, "Heads up!"

Vic and Samuel rumbled through the aisles between the tables. The football flew overhead, being passed from player to player.

A sharp yell of, "Hey! Knock it off!" took the air out of the game, and the ball fell to the floor. Someone picked it up and tossed it underhand to Vic.

Vic caught it, tucked it under his arm, and joined BB and Julie at the table. He sneered, "Well if it isn't Ms. 'I Don't Want to be Bothered' Williams. With the room monitor. I would have thought you'd want a better class of escort." He scooted so his shoulder crowded Julie's.

BB narrowed his eyes. He counted to ten and opened his mouth…

Julie pulled an object from her backpack. "Do you know what a taser looks like, Mr. Shields?"

Vic stared at the device Julie held. Maybe two inches round, four inches long. Quarter-inch prongs on top. Vic's eyes flared. "You wouldn't."

"I most definitely will. Move it over. BB and I were talking." She looked at BB, ignoring Vic. "You were saying a group of you volunteer on Fridays, and you attend church. Who is in this group?" Vic scooted a few respectful inches away.

BB hesitated only a moment. "It's a loose gathering of friends. We've been together since I turned fourteen, so about five years now. We lived together in an eightplex up until November. Then it burned down." *Firebombed in an attempt to kill all of us, but I can save that for a later discussion.* "Now we're scattered around town, but we still get together to volunteer and worship."

Vic sneered, "Yeah, Mr. 'I'm Better Than You.' Doesn't party, doesn't drink, and doesn't like people who do. Just ask him."

BB refused to rise to the bait. "We try to live by the tenet, 'What would Jesus do?' It's not easy, but it's worth it."

Julie motioned to his wrist. "I saw your bracelet."

BB nodded. "My reminder."

Vic snorted. "Because he doesn't remind himself all the time."

Samuel and Leeland brought trays to the table and set them down. Samuel sat opposite Vic. Leeland sat beside Vic. Before Leeland could get settled, Vic grabbed one of the burgers off his plate. Leeland yelped. "Hey! That's mine."

Vic talked around the mouthful of food. "Mine. You owe me. Until we're even, everything you buy belongs to me." He grabbed a handful of the fries to prove his point.

Julie's eyes narrowed, and her face darkened. She glared at Vic. "You are a lowlife, aren't you?"

"I prefer businessman."

Leeland hung his head. "Don't ever borrow money from him. He thinks that means he owns you."

"I do. Until you pay me back, I do."

BB raised his eyebrows at Julie, then nodded to her empty plate. She smiled. "Yes, I'm done."

He picked up both trays and carried them to the receiving window. He returned to the table and asked, "You want to walk and finish this discussion?"

She stood. "Certainly." She picked up her jacket and slipped it on.

Vic stuffed more fries in his mouth. "Ah, and we were just getting to know each other."

Julie frowned at Vic. "I think I know you too well." She rose, pushed her chair in, and followed BB to the exit. They walked out into the well-lit commons. The early spring made the air chilly. As they walked, Julie asked, "Tell me more about your family. Mother, father, sisters, brothers?"

BB grinned. "It's complicated. My dad adopted me when he was twenty-two, and I was fourteen. He adopted my little brother at the same time, who isn't my brother, but I called him that. He was eight. Dad married Wendy in December. No sisters." Explaining the relationships between Wendy and her sister Jen and Wendy's brothers Tav, Luke, and Addison would require a roadmap. Not for the faint at heart. And not on a first "get together."

BB asked, "Do you go to church?" The least invasive way to ask, "Do you know the Lord?"

Julie shook her head. "I haven't found one yet. I am looking, though. Maybe you could recommend one?" She smiled at him.

"Probably." He hesitated. "Would you like to come with me on Sunday? I help my folks with the fosters so they can get to church, too."

"Sure. Herding babies sounds like fun."

BB grinned. "With you helping, it will only be one each. More manageable that way."

BB let Julie lead. She seemed to be heading to one of the dorms across the open field. She pointed to a bench and said, "Maybe we can sit without Vic joining us."

BB grinned. "He does pop up out of nowhere at times. But we'll see him coming. He usually has a posse with him."

Julie groused, "Yeah, his kind never travels alone. Have to have their admirers with them."

BB held his tongue. They sat together on the only slightly damp bench. Julie wrapped her arms around her chest. "I asked you before as a joke, but now I'm serious. How do you live with him as a roommate? It has to be miserable."

"I've learned to let his insults roll off my back." Mostly. "I focus on what Jesus wants me to do, not what Vic is doing."

"You really are into the Lord, aren't you?"

"I try." He touched his bracelet. "It's not for show. It's to remind me."

They sat in silence for several moments. Students passed by, hurrying to leave or hurrying back to the dorms. Some meandered along. All the worlds were in motion. Except BB's.

Julie shivered. BB stood. "You're cold. I'll walk you to your dorm."

"You want to come up for a while? You haven't told me what BB stands for."

BB shook his head. "No. I appreciate it. I'll save that story for the next time we get together."

"And when will that be?" Julie eyed him sideways.

BB thought hard. "I have classes all day tomorrow. And tomorrow night is babysitting with my brother."

Julie shook her head. "Wednesday is my long day, too. I'm free Friday."

BB frowned. "I volunteer at the Mission House on Fridays." He raised his eyebrows. "We can always use more volunteers."

Julie seemed to think about it, then said, "I'll have to let you know. Give me your cell number, and I'll text you."

They exchanged information. Julie eyed him again. "You sure you don't want to come up for a while? I do have roommates." She laughed. "I lied about living by myself."

BB shook his head. "No. I'm sure. I'll wait to hear from you." He smiled. "I'm glad we got to talk. Good night."

He watched her walk into the dorm, then sighed. What had he learned?

Julie could be a friend, but beyond that? Maybe not with the invitation to come to her dorm room. He would need to be very careful with the relationship. If they had one. Still, there might be possibilities…

He turned and walked back to his dorm. BB heard the music coming from the room before he left the elevator. If there were a time to talk, now would be it. Before his roommates became intoxicated…or too intoxicated to remember what they were talking about.

He slipped in his card, typed in the code, and went in.

Samuel and Vic sat at the table. Two girls sat on the bed. They held a bottle of vodka and passed it back and forth. Leeland sat at his desk, trying to look like he wasn't upset about not being a part of the party. His face drooped. His eyes were clouded over. He had an open bottle of cheap rum and poured some of the contents into a cup. A can of soda sat on the desk beside him.

Vic called out, "Hey, BB. You made it to the party. Did Ms. Williams dump you already?"

BB picked up his books from his desk. "No party. You know I don't go for coed situations. I'll be back tomorrow."

Vic threw a hand in the air. "Ah, come on. We're going to have fun."

"I doubt it." BB grabbed some clothes from his dresser and started out the door.

Leeland called, "Hey, BB. Where you going?"

BB started to respond, but Vic interrupted him. "I bet he's going home to Mommy." He guffawed. The girls tittered.

Samuel threw a pillow at Vic. "At least he has one who'll talk to him."

Vic cursed and slammed the bottle on the table, sloshing the contents. He had a few choice things to say about his parents BB had to filter through the Holy Spirit. He waited until Vic finished his tirade, then said, "I'll see you guys tomorrow. When you're sober, we'll talk."

Leeland's voice sounded morose. "That's never."

BB didn't answer. Leeland wasn't far wrong. BB walked out of the room and headed for his car. Where would he go? He could go home, of course. But was that the answer? He climbed into his SUV and sat behind the wheel. "Lord, what do You want me to do? I can't stay. Not with girls there. I know You want me to be an influence, and I want to be. But I can't stay when they're partying." Not with women around.

Addison lived close by. He texted him. *You got a free couch?*

The answer came back almost immediately. *For you? Always.*

Yeah.

Come on down.

Thx.

Addison graduated a year ago. He'd be a good one to talk to. BB started the engine, put the car in gear, and headed to the youngest Vaughn's condo. The twenty-minute drive would clear his head and maybe give him insight.

Or not. Addison waited at the door as BB let himself in. They hugged, and then Addison led the way into the dining area. "Something to drink?"

BB snorted. "Dad's coffee."

"Sorry, but I don't keep mud in my house. Mick will have to come over and fix it for you."

They both snickered. BB shook his head. "Dad's too busy fixing baby bottles." They walked into the Spartan living area. A couch, a recliner, and a coffee table. Pictures on the wall of the Knights of the Octagon, taken before the fire. A slight tang of antiseptic tickled the air.

BB sat on the leather couch while his adoptive uncle/brother took the recliner. Addison leaned forward and seemed to study BB. "What's going on?"

"Girls in the room. Looks like it will be an all-night party."

Addison scowled. "I gotcha, man. What are you going to do about it?"

"Sleep on your couch tonight. I need to talk to the guys

about respect, but the time never seems right."

Addison nodded. "It won't ever 'be' right. You have to make it right."

"Did you come up against this?" BB splayed his fingers and tapped them together.

Addison leaned back in his chair. "At first, from the other side. I wasn't part of the Knights when I started school." He massaged his damaged arm. The motorcycle accident took most of the function from his arm and leg. As well as his starting quarterback career. Arrogance will do that to you. But God had redeemed Addison if not his physical prowess.

BB nodded. "I know. I hadn't met you then."

"I don't know how I'd have handled someone like you." Addison rubbed the arm of the chair. "In my insolent days, I might have been like your roommates."

"Would you have listened to anything I had to say?" BB tipped his head to the side.

"Not if you preached at me. But living your faith? I might have respected that."

"Would you respect me not partying with you? Not drinking and welcoming the girls? Do I need to stay in the room?"

Addison leaned forward again. "My sense would be it spoke louder when you left. Would I do the same thing now? Yes. Absolutely. Compromising your values to make yourself 'one of them' isn't what Jesus did. He never strayed from Who He was."

"How do I get them to listen? To at least respect my space? I'm not telling them not to drink. I'd prefer they didn't smoke weed when I'm there. I'm not saying they can or they can't. Or should or shouldn't. I only want them to respect my…my being there." *My existence.*

Addison shrugged. "You have to talk to them, BB. You have to make the time."

BB frowned. "I'd get more attention from Dad's

babies." He laid his hands on the coffee table.

"Maybe that's how you need to think about them. Babies. They're lost boys. Jesus sent you to lead them to Him."

BB shook his head. "I'm not the one. Vic is the leader, and he doesn't respect me. Or anything about me." He sat back and rubbed his knee. It didn't hurt, but it gave him something to do.

Addison gave a straight-lipped smile. "Then you know where to start."

BB grumbled. "I knew you were going to say that."

Addison laughed. "And that's why you called me. So I could tell you what you already knew. Confirmation." The man's eyes sparkled.

"Right. It wasn't what I wanted you to say."

"Probably not." Addison held up his left hand, displaying the ban on his wrist. "Never promised it would be easy."

BB added the maxim, "But it will be worth it in the end. I know. I know. Can I still sleep here tonight?" He couldn't keep the plaintive note from his voice.

Addison waved to the couch. "It's all yours, brother. What time do you need to get up?"

BB pulled out his phone. "I'll shower, change, and be out of here by seven."

"No rush. I'm not in the office tomorrow." Addison grinned. He looked at his phone, probably to remind himself what he had planned.

BB chuckled. "How is it going for you?" He hadn't had a serious talk with Addison in the last month. They needed to catch up.

"Trying to maintain the trafficking rescue and not look like a millionaire is tough." Addison shook his head. "If it gets out I have wealth, I'll lose my credibility on the streets."

BB agreed. "Going to school on a fake scholarship so no one knows I'm paying for it myself from Granddad

Quinn's millions isn't easy either."

Addison ducked his head. "First world problems. Having wealth and living like we don't have it."

"But that's what we all prayed about. How not to let the ten million apiece change us. Or change our decisions to follow Jesus." *And none of us knew how hard it would be. Except Popdad Quinn, who's been doing it for years. He knew. And we're all taking lessons from him.*

Addison chuckled. "Oh, it changed us. All of us. We're in hiding. Keeping our wealth secret so we can do our alms in private. Not easy."

BB picked up a pillow from the trio on the floor. "I hear you." He hesitated. "Speaking of alms…one of my roommates is in hock to Vic. Dude is a regular loan shark. Says he owns Leeland. I'm thinking about paying his debt. Anonymously."

Addison cocked his head. "How are you going to arrange that?"

"Thought about sliding some money into his dresser or in his wallet, but I'm not sure he wouldn't find something else to spend it on. I haven't worked out the details yet. I could slip it to a friend to give to him, but Leeland doesn't have many friends." BB trailed off in thought. This could be harder than it looked. It sounded so simple in his head. How would he pay off the debt without anyone knowing it was him?

Addison brought up a second objection. "And when he goes back in debt? How many times will you bail him out?"

"How many times has the Lord bailed me out?"

Addison shifted in his chair. "I think you're missing the point. Proverbs says if you bail out a fool, you'll have to do it over and over again. Jesus made one sacrifice for all sins for all time. He didn't have to die over and over every time we screwed up."

BB considered the point. He looked at Addison and asked, "Then how do I help him?"

"Maybe you set up a scholarship for him. One that comes with a budget."

BB mulled it over. "I could do that. I've already got three others on secret scholarships. I can do one more. And see if he can stick to the budget."

"How are your others doing?" Addison raised his eyebrows.

"One walks close to the credit line. One's been over it a time or two. And one stays as far from debt as possible. I'm trying to find a way to help her be a little less frugal without interfering."

Addison laughed. "You'll figure it out." He stood and pointed to the closet. "You know where the sheets are." Addison tapped his knuckles with BB and walked into his bedroom, closing the door behind him.

BB retrieved the sheets and blankets and made up the couch. He didn't bother pulling out the bed but made himself comfortable on the cushions. He'd get a good night's sleep. Tomorrow would be another chance to seek reconciliation with the roomies. And help Leeland free himself from Vic's clutches.

BB kneeled beside the couch, calmed his mind, and prayed, "Lord, if I'm failing You, show me how to do Your will. Please show me how to impact Samuel, Vic, and Leeland. Meet the needs they have and bring them to Yourself. Only Your Spirit can make a heart change. Be with Dad, Wendy, Ben, and the babies. They need You."

Vic, Samuel, and Leeland need Me.

BB nodded. "I know, Lord. And I'm trying to be Your ambassador."

Do you love them as much as you love the fosters? I do.

BB sat back on his haunches. He hadn't thought about it that way. He should love them the same. Jesus certainly did. Instead of avoiding conflict with his roommates, maybe he should try serving them. Loving them. Like Jesus did. Does.

BB whispered, "Show me how, Father. I'll do better, Lord. With Your help, I will." He heard his dad's voice. *Always end with you love Him. And always mean it.*

BB smiled. "I love You, Lord."

He climbed onto the couch, stretched out, and slept.

* * *

WEDNESDAY

Well?
This may be more difficult than we thought.
I don't want to hear difficult. I want results.
I need time.
You have one week.

BB left Addison's place in time to get to his first class. It would be noon before he made it back to the dorm. Everyone should have cleared out by then. He would have time to marshal his arguments and defense before Leeland, Vic, and Samuel returned.

Love your enemies. Do good to those who persecute and badly use you.

BB sighed. "I hear You. Show me what I need to do to love them enough so they see You."

Leeland needed help. There were ways…when he returned to the dorm, he'd email Leeland about the scholarship he'd been awarded. For what remained a mystery. Drawn by a lottery from current first-year students. Random. Leeland's lucky day. Paying off Vic would be even better.

At noon, BB opened the door. A heavy scent of "Black Opium" perfume floated from the room. A figure lay under the covers on the top bunk. His bunk. Not a large figure. Not a child, either. BB backed out of the door and leaned against the cinder block wall. He slowed his breathing to keep from hyperventilating. This went beyond a joke. This…this…

This was the guys at their worst. Like he'd been before he met Jesus. No difference. Deal with it in love.

Wise as serpents, harmless as doves.

BB tiptoed back into the room and set his books down. He drew in a deep breath. What would Jesus do? What would his dad and the Knights do? What did he want to do?

Storm in and raise a scene. Yank her—assuming it was a her—out of his bunk and chase her out of the room.

Now he knew what he *wouldn't* do…what about a real plan?

BB powered up his laptop and made sure the camera had been turned on. And the microphone. He made sure he was recording, then slipped back out. He'd go to the library and wait another hour. Maybe Addison knew a way to access all the secret information remotely? It would be worth a call. BB might need it.

Could he be accused of spying on the guys? Was it spying if they knew you had a camera and recorder sitting in plain sight? They had them, too. Everyone did. Just because they didn't know you could use them that way…that could be construed as their problem.

Couldn't it? BB would chase that rabbit down its hole later. Right now, he needed the backup.

He got voicemail. "Addison, yeah. Listen. The camera information you showed me how to access. Is there a remote component to it? Like, can I pull it to my phone and see it? And hear it? I may need it for evidence. Call me."

BB strode to the library. Anger flooded him. His steps pounded the ground. He knew this had to be Vic's doing. Had to be. The question remained, did Leeland and Samuel have a part in it? If they did, Leeland could find his way out from under Vic's thumb. He didn't deserve help.

A still, soft voice whispered in his head. *Did you?*

BB slowed his pace. Stopped. Exhaled. Breathed in. Exhaled. Prayed, "I hear You, Lord. I do. Show me what You want me to do. I need to move out, right? This is the last line in the sand. They put a woman in my bed. Someone did. I can't do this, Lord. I can't. I'll stay friends and try to help Leeland, but this is more than I can do."

His phone rang. Addison. His uncle's voice sounded concerned. "What's going on, BB? What happened?"

"There's a woman in my bed. Or I'm pretty sure it's a woman. And I need to deal with it. I need to see what's going on before I go in there, and I need to have proof I didn't do anything when I *do* go in there."

Addison fell silent for several seconds. "I see. Don't suppose you could have the dorm manager roust her, could you?"

"It's not against school policy to fraternize. It's against Coach's policy to party. Samuel and Vic could get kicked off the team if he finds out about last night's drinking. Especially since they're all underage." *Might serve them right. Except losing your future for one stupid prank is extreme. I can't do that to them.*

Addison hesitated. "Any chance Samuel doesn't know about it? And gets caught in Vic's game?"

BB scowled and kicked an errant dandelion. "Then Vic gets off again? Like always?"

"The Judge of all the earth knows how to hold the guilty accountable."

BB sagged. "Of which I am one. I know." He slowed his steps to the library.

"You were. There is no condemnation now. Remember that before you start thinking the enemy's lies." Addison paused. "Those remote instructions you need? Go to settings."

BB followed while his uncle rattled off commands and codes. He reached the doors of the student entrance to the library as Addison finished. BB put in the last command and saw a clear shot of his dorm room. The laptop camera had a wide-angle lens that covered the bunks and the desk. He would see everything...and maybe too much. He'd shut down anything he didn't need to see. *Lord? Mercy, please. And grace. I'm not a voyeur. I don't want to be. I want this stunt to be over. Help me.*

"Thanks, Addison. I appreciate your help. Sorry for needing it so often."

"We'll talk about setting limits and boundaries later." Addison chuckled. "Praying for you, BB." The phone went dead.

BB found a quiet place in an alcove to do his surveillance. He set up his books and notes and tried to look like he was working on his studies. All the while studying his phone.

Twenty minutes passed, and movement on the remote viewer caught his eye. BB watched as the figure on his bed rolled off the top bunk. She was clad. Not with much, but she was clad. He breathed a silent *Thank You.* He didn't recognize the woman. Another relief.

She stretched, then retrieved a phone from the desk. She punched in a number. "Yeah, Vic. It's almost two o'clock. You said he'd be here by noon. I don't care. I'm not spending all afternoon waiting to 'surprise' your friend. My rates went up at one."

She huffed. "Don't get cheeky with me. I don't care what you're offering."

BB could see a look of disgust on the woman's face. "You don't own me, mister. I've got better friends than your football buddies. They carry a bigger stick. You got that? So don't go threatening me." There came a pause. "No. Not gonna do it. Game's up at two." She disconnected the call.

BB's phone pinged. Text message. Vic. *Need a favor. Need you to get my jacket from my locker. Coach is doing an inspection. Bring it to me at the field before two.*

BB stared at the message. How to answer. Sorry, can't

make it? Sorry, your trick won't work? Sure, Vic, I'll go. After two.

Scenarios ran through his head. After the tenth one, he prayed, "What do you want me to do, Lord?" He lowered his head and listened. And listened. And smiled.

He typed, Can't make the field by two. Will get to the room by then and will bring it as soon as I can. Does that still work?

ASAP. Sooner is better.

I hear you. BB shook his head. "Boy, do I hear you." He strolled across the commons back to the dorm. He arrived at the door as a woman exited. She wore a midriff halter top and tight blue jeans. She looked to be in her mid-twenties.

BB smiled at her. "Hello." He made sure to hold the door open. Wide open.

She tapped her finger on his cheek. "You missed all the fun."

BB shrugged. "That's okay. I'm not a party person."

She looked him up and down. "If I weren't in a hurry, I'd see if I could change that. You look like you could be a joy to play with."

BB stepped back to give her a broad berth. "Have a good day."

She smiled at him. Her eyes narrowed but sparkled. She brushed past him as she sauntered down the hall to the elevator. She did not look back.

BB sighed. "Thank You, Lord. Tell me what You want me to say or do." He grabbed Vic's jacket from the man's locker and headed for the fieldhouse. Dodged another one.

* * *

Ben sat alone at the lunch table. No art supplies. He would not be singled out again for drawing people. He finished his lunch and went outside to hang near the door to the hall of his next class. Students weren't allowed in the halls during lunch. Not without permission. Ben lounged against the brick wall and waited for the bell to ring.

Tricia approached him. Her eyes were narrowed, her face scrunched into a scowl. She stopped in front of Ben. She planted her fists on her side and accused, "You drew a picture of me, didn't you? Without my permission. You can't do that. Don't you ever do it again."

Ben frowned. "I won't. I've got better people to draw." The lie hurt him.

Tricia wasn't finished. "And Craig is saying you have a crush on me. And that I like you. You're lying. You want attention, that's all. You're not gonna get it from me."

Ben snorted. "I don't want your attention. I don't even like you. I love you because Jesus says I have to. But I never told anyone I liked you. Craig made all that stuff up."

Tricia stared at him for a moment. She took a step back and eyed him. "You know about Jesus?"

"I know Jesus." Ben knew the difference.

"Where do you go to church?" Tricia lost her anger. Her face softened.

"Sometimes we go to the Downtown Mission. Other times, we go to Galt Community Church. It's over on the west side of town. By the river." Everyone knew about the Mission.

"Who's we?"

"My family."

Tricia leaned against the wall next to Ben. "Yeah? Like who?"

"My adopted dad and mom, and my brother. Sometimes, we take the foster babies."

"You have foster kids?" Tricia's eyes widened, and she cocked her head.

Ben nodded. "Yeah. We have four foster babies right now. Three are triplets, and one is by herself."

Tricia tossed her head. "Triplets? That's so cool. But that's a lot of babies. Why are your parents doing that?"

Ben shrugged. "Jesus told us to help the orphans. We're trying to do what He says." He fingered the bracelet he wore.

"It says 'WWJD.' It means—"

"I know what it means. I've seen it before. I didn't know anybody cared about it, though." She tossed her hair behind her shoulders.

"We do." Ben stared at the ground, then looked up. "Where do you go?"

"When I'm with my mom, I go to Smithfield. When I'm with my dad, I don't go."

"He doesn't go to church?"

"He goes. I don't. I'm old enough to make up my own mind, and I decided not to go."

She wasn't any older than Ben. Her parents must be apart. Divorced? That's sad. A thought hit him. "Is that why you miss so much school? You're with your dad?"

"Yeah. Half the time I'm with him and go to a private school. Mom didn't like the arrangement, but that's what the court decided."

How would it be to go to two schools? Going to a different school after four years in private school had been hard enough. "How does that work?"

"I'm with Dad from July through November. Mom has me from January through May. They alternate June and December."

"Must be hard."

"It is." The bell for class rang. Tricia grabbed Ben's arm before he could go. "If you ever draw a picture of me, I want to see it, okay? But when no one is around. And I get to keep it."

Ben nodded. "Deal." Tricia ran to her classroom. Ben strolled to his. Women. He'd never understand them. He made a mental note to draw Tricia tonight. Just for her.

* * *

BB, Samuel, Vic, and Leeland walked back to the room from the fieldhouse. The air felt crisp. Lilac bushes perfumed the air. Students walked a little faster to get from one place to another. BB started the conversation. "I want to talk about our living arrangement."

Vic snorted. "Nothing wrong with it, except you're a drudge on the fun."

"A woman in my bed goes beyond fun. I'd like to know what I can do so you respect my presence." BB kept his cool. And the Lord sat on his tongue.

Vic snapped, "Move out." He flung his jacket over his shoulder.

BB looked at Samuel and Leeland. "You want me out?"

Samuel fell silent for a moment, then he shook his head. "No, man. It's cool you being there. I got no problem with it." He lifted both hands in the air.

Leeland refused to look at Vic. "I don't see a problem with you there." He raised his head. "It's your room, too." He held Vic's eyes in challenge.

Vic growled. "Your interest rate just went up."

Leeland glared at Vic. "You'd find a reason to raise it no matter what I do. What's the difference?" He narrowed his eyes and stared hard at the football star.

"I'll own you till you die, sucker." Vic sneered.

BB asked, "How much do you owe him?" Heat ran through BB's tone.

Vic shook his head. "More than you'll ever have." Contempt.

BB turned to Vic and demanded. "How much? Interest and all. Right now, not five minutes from now." BB pointed at the ground. "How much does he owe?"

"Why?" Suspicion filled the question.

"How much?" BB put more heat in his voice. "Answer the question." He'd end this charade now.

Vic narrowed his gaze. He looked to the side, looked at the ground, then said, "Five hundred dollars."

Leeland's jaw dropped, "What? I never borrowed that much."

"Interest, dude. Interest. Compounded daily. That's how banks make their millions." He gave a straight-lipped smirk. "Learned it in Economics 101."

BB ignored the interplay. "Five hundred. Does that include today's interest?"

Vic eyed BB sideways. "Let's say it does."

"Does it or doesn't it? Yes or no." He was done playing games.

Vic stopped walking and turned to face BB. "Since you're so interested in this loser, yes, that includes today's interest. Five hundred. What are you going to do about it?"

BB turned to Leeland. "I know a scholarship program you can get on that will pay room, board, books, and give you money to live on. And teach you to budget your money. They give loans and forgive debts when you put in the effort to learn. I can hook you up with it tomorrow."

Leeland's eyes widened. "How come I never heard of it before?"

"It's a private company. They don't advertise. But I have an in with them and can get you on the program. If you're interested." BB turned to Samuel. "Open to you, too, if you want."

Samuel shook his head. "I'll do it on my own or not at all. No one is paying my way for anything. If I can't afford it, I'll do without." Misplaced pride burned in his eyes.

BB looked back at Leeland. "You interested?" He needed to know before he gave Vic the money.

"Yes." A few more descriptive phrases went with the affirmation.

BB ignored them. "Fine. I'll show you the links to apply tomorrow." He reached into his pocket and pulled out his wallet. He extracted six one-hundred-dollar bills and handed them to Vic. "There. He's paid off. You don't own him anymore."

Leeland's eyes exploded in his head. "What? You're joking."

Vic laughed. "Right. It's counterfeit. Fake. I know better." He held the bills up to examine them.

"Take it to the bank. It's all real. So is the deal I just made. Leeland is clear with you. No more owning him. I paid for his freedom."

BB started walking to the room again. Leeland rushed to keep up with him. Samuel followed a few steps behind. Vic stood in the same spot.

Leeland grabbed BB's arm stopping his forward progress. "You didn't have to do that."

BB nodded. "Yeah, I did. Someone had to. You said it yourself. Once Vic gets his hooks in, he never lets go. Well, he has no power over you now." BB stepped out again.

Leeland stared at the ground. "What do I owe you?" His voice sounded dejected.

BB stopped walking and faced Leeland. "Nothing. Absolutely nothing. We're square. I bailed you out because you couldn't help yourself. That's it. No other reason."

Leeland stared off at the dorm building. "Do I have to go to church with you? Have to listen to you preach?" Dejection was tempered with concern.

"No more than you did before I paid Vic." Which meant never, but BB didn't mention what Leeland already knew.

Samuel caught up. BB knew he'd been listening to the conversation. BB told Leeland, "I did it because Someone paid for my freedom, once."

Leeland rolled his eyes. "And you're going to tell me about it, right?"

"Not unless you ask me. I told you, there are no strings attached. No markers to call in. You're free, Leeland. After I get you set up for the scholarship, you're still free. You can take it or leave it. Abuse it or use it. It doesn't matter. I won't say anything, no matter what. This is a one-time good deal."

Samuel kept his voice low. "Vic won't let this go, you know. He likes having a servant. Bought and paid for. You freeing Leeland isn't going to set well."

BB chuckled. "Yeah, I know how that goes. I'm ready for him." After the woman in the bed trick, BB was ready for almost anything.

Vic joined the group at the elevator. He punched Leeland hard in the upper arm. "Sorry to see you go. But I'm sure you'll be back. You're a loser. Even on some fancy scholarship, you'll still need me. But you better believe the interest rates will be even higher."

Leeland rubbed his shoulder. "You've got the last of my money. I won't be needing yours again."

"We'll see. I know you better. Mr. Money Pockets thinks he's done something wonderful, but you'll be back. Then we'll see how deep his pockets go." He glared at BB and added, "And I still want you gone."

Leeland said, "I vote he stays." He stood a little taller, with more conviction in his voice.

Samuel studied Vic a moment, then nodded. "I think he should stay. I vote he does." He raised his eyebrows at Vic. "Remember, I'm the one blocking for you. I could miss an assignment, and you'd get leveled. Just a thought."

Vic glared hard at Samuel but gritted his teeth and acknowledged, "He stays."

BB pushed the button to the fifth floor. "No more having someone steal my stuff. No more putting women in my bed." He pushed one step further. "No more weed when I'm studying."

Vic stepped into the elevator. "Who are you to say what I can do?" He sneered his question.

"I'm asking you to respect my presence. You can smoke all the weed you want, but not when I'm in the room. That's what I'm saying. Please."

"Oooo…please. Now you're begging." Vic hooted as they rode up the floors.

"Not begging. Just being respectful." There was so much he wanted to say…so much he almost said. But being snarky or angry wouldn't earn him any points with Vic or the Lord. Still, he had to convince Vic on the earthly plane.

Samuel bumped Vic's shoulder. "Come on, Vic. He's a

good roommate to have. He doesn't leave stuff lying around, and he showers on a regular basis. He doesn't drink your liquor or steal your weed. We could do a lot worse."

Vic seemed to consider Samuel's arguments. As they exited the elevator, Vic said, "Fine. I'll consider it."

BB pressed, "No, you'll agree to it. No weed when I'm studying." He'd fight one battle at a time. Maybe it wasn't the highest order, but any respect would be a significant victory.

"Fine. No weed. But no hanging around so I don't smoke it."

BB assured him, "I don't hang around. I'm here working on classwork, or I'm sleeping. That's it."

"Fine." Vic made each word an insult. "I'll respect your presence."

"Thank you." BB did not extend his hand. He knew when to stop. Dad had taught him well.

* * *

WEDNESDAY EVENING

Ben sat on the couch at home. He listened to Dad and Wendy talking in the kitchen. They were having a cup of coffee before they went to church. Before they all went to church. Ben waited until they came into the living room. "I'm not going to church." He sat on the couch, his knee bouncing.

Dad's eyes widened, and his eyebrows went up. Never a good sign when Dad's eyebrows went up. "Excuse me?" Dad's voice rose on the "me." Also not a good sign.

Ben repeated his declaration. "I'm not going to church." He pushed ahead. "I'm old enough to make up my own mind. I'm staying home." He pressed his hand against his knee to stop it from jumping.

Dad did nothing but stare at Ben. No words. He didn't say yes, no, or what do you mean? He stared.

Ben sat on his hands. "Tricia said she could make up her mind. She said she's old enough. She's the same age I am."

Dad nodded. "You're old enough to make up your mind. But you're not old enough to stay home from church. While you live here, as part of this family, you do what the family does."

Dad stopped. He drew in a deep breath. He looked at Wendy. She shook her head. He cocked his. She nodded.

Dad gave her a single nod. He looked at Ben again. "You want to go on vacations with us, right?"

Ben nodded. "Yes." He would never say, "Yeah." He always said, "Yes." He loved Dad. He respected him.

"You want to go to restaurants and dinners, correct?" Dad began counting on his fingers.

"Yes." Ben shifted on the couch. Something was coming.

"You want to come with us to see Quinn and Grace and any of the other Knights, right?"

"Yes." Always. Dad headed down a path Ben didn't want to travel.

"You want to go with us to see BB?"

He tried protesting. "But those are all things I want to do. I don't want to go to church."

"Tell me why. What has Jesus done that makes you not want to obey Him?"

Ben scowled. That wasn't what he thought Dad would say. "I want to obey Him. I don't want to go to church."

Dad leaned against the wall. Wendy moved to the living room and sat in her chair. She glanced at the clock. Dad shook his head. Wendy nodded.

They were talking to each other without saying a word. Adults could do that. Especially married adults. Uncle Tav and Aunt Jen did it all the time. They got married at the same time Dad and Wendy did. Ben squirmed.

Dad's voice remained calm and even. He said, "Going to church is part of obeying Jesus. We come together to show Him we love Him. And we gather to encourage each other. Ralph and Meg always look forward to you being there. You help them get into the building."

Ralph had a wheelchair. Meg was blind and needed help. Ben loved helping them. They told him he was the best thing to happen to their day. He would miss them if he didn't go.

"And Crystal loves it when you help her in the

preschool class. You're her number one helper."

She always said the same thing. She needed his help with the little boys. He liked helping her. He liked it when the boys would hug him in the hall. They'd pull their parents and say, "He's my teacher."

And he liked singing to Jesus. Jesus had given Ben his parents, and his brother, and his home. Jesus had given him Life. Why wouldn't he want to go to church?

Because Tricia didn't go? That made no sense. Ben liked church.

Would Tricia like Ben if he went?

Did it matter?

Well, yeah, it did. Shouldn't it?

Should it?

No. What mattered was Jesus. Right?

He took a deep breath and lifted his head. "I'm going to church. I want to go, and I'm going." He stood.

Dad smiled. Mostly with his eyes. "Thank you, Ben. You made a good choice."

Ben corrected his dad. "I made the right choice."

Dad put his arm around Ben's shoulders. "Yes, you did. Let's wrap up these babies before they decide they don't want to go. BB should be waiting for us." He moved to gather the babies and their things. Lots of things. Blankets and binkies and bottles and booties and diapers. Lots of diapers.

Ben laughed. "Yeah, babies don't know how to make good choices."

Wendy's eyes shone brightly. She was happy. She came over and kissed him on top of the head. "Thanks, Ben."

He hugged her. "I love you, Wendy."

"Love you, Ben."

* * *

THURSDAY

Walking back from his last afternoon class, BB looked at his phone. He had a text from Julie. *I'd like to join you at the Mission tomorrow. What time, and can you pick me up?*

He smiled, and typed back, *Seven a.m. and sure. We'll serve the breakfast crowd. Where do I pick you up?*

Dorm 20. Room 355. Come on up.

I'll wait for you at the front and keep the heat running.

I don't bite.

BB sighed. *Can't do it. Will wait at the door.*

Fine. I'll see you then.

This could get complicated. If Julie continued…

"One day at a time, right, Lord? Tomorrow's trouble is for tomorrow." Today's trouble wasn't over. He texted Vic. *Coming up.* Let's see if the agreement holds.

BB anticipated a problem. He wasn't disappointed. Vic's text read, *Give me twenty minutes.*

Twenty minutes to finish a cigarette? *Ten. Open the door and windows.*

Vic responded with a few cutting remarks. BB ignored them. He hung around the lobby of the dorm for ten minutes. Watched students running through the halls. Probably late for dinner or class. Lack of planning. If they just…

A silent nudge cut off the judgment. Remembrances of him being late more than once in his short life bowed his head. *Sorry, Lord.*

He arrived at the room. The door had been opened as he'd requested. He stepped inside and looked around. Vic lounged on his bunk. Samuel sat at his desk, working on classwork. Leeland leaned his chair against the wall on two feet, reading. Or appearing to read. BB glanced around the room to ensure there were no additional bodies.

Looked safe. No suspicious lumps in his—or anyone else's—bed. The air held the slight aroma of weed, but it seemed to be clearing. At least he knew he wouldn't get high from the leftover smoke. A window had been pulled open, and a cool breeze circulated the air.

He moved to his desk, set his books down, and turned to face Vic. "Thanks for doing what I asked. I appreciate it."

Vic snorted. "You owe me."

BB corrected, "I owe you consideration. That's what you'll get in return."

Vic sat in his bunk. "Consideration. So, if I want to have a friend spend the night, you'll loan me your bed."

BB shook his head. "No. No one sleeps in my bunk but me. I'll leave for a few hours so you and your 'friend' can have time together. But I'm not staying out all night for you."

Samuel looked up from his studies. "That's fair. That's fair for all of us."

Leeland threw in, "Except you two aren't supposed to be partying, remember? Coach's rules."

Vic made some disparaging remarks about the coach and his rules. He glared at Leeland. "Just because somebody bought you doesn't mean you get to make comments about my life."

Leeland scowled and turned back to his reading.

BB raised his eyebrows. "You don't have to be on the team. You can get a scholarship without playing football."

Vic added a few more choice words. "What am I going to do after college, huh? If I don't play ball, I don't have a future."

Samuel shrugged. "Every player I know has a career plan that doesn't include a lifetime of football. Sooner or later, you got to retire." He looked pointedly at Vic and raised his eyebrows.

BB added, "Or you get hurt and end your career. Happens to lots of players."

Vic stretched out on his bed, his hands behind his head. "Not me. I'm the golden boy. Just ask my dad. He'll tell you. We've got it all planned out."

BB shook his head. "Good luck with that." He looked to Samuel. "Have you found out anything more about the student who died?"

Samuel nodded. "I heard there's some question about the note. The police are looking into it."

"Question about the note?"

"Yeah. I don't know the whole story. I only know the police are investigating. There may be more to the affair than we first thought."

BB pulled out his English book and turned to the appropriate section. Sounded like an intrigue he didn't want to be involved in. *Lord, You know the situation. Use this tragedy for Your purpose. Only You can, Lord.* Out of the corner of his eye, he saw Vic pull out his phone and tap the screen.

Music, loud enough to rattle the windows, blared from the speakers over his bed. BB put on his noise-canceling headphones. He could still hear the faint rhythm of the bass but nothing else. He continued studying.

He felt the reverberations of someone pounding on the wall. He ignored it. Vic could fight it out with the neighbors. Samuel got up and closed the door, then closed the window. BB doubted it would contain the noise, but it was a start. Dorm life.

FRIDAY

What progress have you made?
It's taking time. He's not like the others.
All men are the same. Do the deed.
You don't think I'm trying? I know what's at stake.
Then get it done.
Trust me.

BB waited for Julie to come down at Dorm 20's front door. He lounged against the cinder block wall, watching women and men straggle into the commons. He'd arrived before seven on the off-chance Julie would be early. He could hope.

Julie came out of the door right at seven. She smiled at BB. "Morning, Mr. BB. Oh, no, it's Andres. BB is the mysterious first name."

BB felt a tinge of heat rush to his cheeks. He motioned for Julie to walk with him. "It's not mysterious. It's a family story, that's all."

"And we have the morning for you to tell me." Her eyes sparkled with amusement.

BB led Julie to his vehicle, a dark blue four-door SUV. The color had been his one extravagant part of the purchase. That, and the heated seats. Otherwise, he blended in with every other SUV on the road. No show of overindulgence here. He opened the door for Julie. She did not protest. BB breathed a slight sigh of relief. One anticipated battle down.

As BB put the car in motion, Julie asked, "Can we stop and get a coffee?"

BB shook his head. "Unless you can drink it before we get there, no. Management doesn't like us to bring in outside food. It reinforces the difference between us and those using the Mission. We're 'privileged.' We want there to be no divide." He grinned. "You can drink as much of the Mission coffee as you like. If my dad makes it, it'll be as strong as an espresso, believe me."

Julie's eyes narrowed slightly, then returned to normal. She adjusted her seatbelt across her chest. "This will be interesting."

BB looked at the road. "Do you still want to come?"

"Of course I do. I'm not that shallow."

Warmth trickled into his cheeks again. "I didn't think you were. We don't know each other all that well." *Or as well as I'd like to. Yet.*

"So, help me get to know you. What does the BB stand for?"

"Ben's brother." BB glanced across for Julie's reaction.

She eyed him sideways. "What?" Her jaw opened.

BB stopped for a school bus. He waited until the driver retracted the STOP sign, then started again. He nodded. "Ben and I were kids up in the hills. Way back in the sticks. We were fosters. He wasn't even my brother at the time."

Another bus. Another wait.

"We were being cared for by a man named Pete. Cared for is a fairly loose interpretation of what went on. But Pete got murdered, and I took Ben and ran into the hills. I was afraid the people who killed Pete would come back after us and kill us, too."

BB maneuvered around the bus and pulled ahead of traffic. "We camped in the hills for a couple of months, living by the river." BB turned down a narrow alley, watched for obstacles that would take his mirrors off, and turned another corner.

"Then we ran into Dad and his bunch of friends. They rescued us…well, technically, we rescued them. Ben didn't talk at the time, and they didn't know what to call him. Since he'd helped save them, they called him 'Ben.' Short for 'Benefactor.'"

BB pulled into the parking lot of a much-worn church that had seen better days. The upstairs windows were boarded shut. Some of the first-level windows had cardboard in them. The entrance had a hand-written sign over the door that said, "Downtown Mission." People who had seen better days lined up waiting to get in and get a hot meal. Some were families. Some were older couples. Some were singles. No one who wanted a meal would be turned away.

Julie eyed BB. "Okay, you've explained Ben. What about you?"

"At the time, I didn't want to tell them my real name. So I told them to call me BB, for 'Ben's Brother.' They called me that so much and for so long it stuck. When Dad made the adoption official, I had them change my name legally to BB." He smiled. "Now you're one of a very few who know my deepest, darkest secret."

Julie laughed. "If that's your darkest secret, you've lived a sheltered life."

BB stretched his back. There were more than a few family secrets left to not tell. *How about I was determined to murder the ones who murdered Pete? Will that pass for a dark secret? Or there have been hired guns trying to assassinate us multiple times? Popdad worked for the Office? No, there are a few other stories we won't discuss.*

BB said nothing more. He got out and went to open Julie's door. She pushed it wide and smiled. "You can open the door to let me in, but I'm quite capable of opening it to get out, thank you."

He nodded and waited for her to exit the vehicle. She

rose and stepped out. He closed the door and pointed to a walkway around the building, marked by faded white paint. "We go in the back, so no one thinks we're cutting in line."

"Is that a problem? Are people so petty?" Julie hmphed.

"Some are. Especially when they're afraid the food will run out before it's their turn." Hadn't happened yet. Never would if he could help it.

They followed the path around to the rear of the building. Tendrils of 'just now coming to life' vines dropped from the gutters. Heads of flowering bulbs of some variety stuck through the dark soil along the blacktop. Someone tried to beautify the space whether anyone noticed or not.

The back door stood open. BB led Julie past classrooms with brightly painted walls and repurposed tables and benches. The hall had children's artwork everywhere. "Jesus Loves Me" seemed to be the primary theme.

They entered the kitchen, where volunteers bustled to prepare breakfast meals for the hungry crowd. BB pointed out a bald man directing traffic. "Pastor DeWayne. He runs the place."

BB intercepted the man before he could leave the kitchen. "Dee. Meet Julie Williams. She's here to help."

DeWayne's face broke into a giant smile. "Fresh blood! Fantastic! Welcome, Julie. BB, take her to the lunch line. Your folks are there."

The man disappeared into the cafeteria in a breathless rush.

Julie eyed BB with curiosity. And a measure of discomfort. "What was that?"

"Pastor DeWayne. The end of the day is the only time you'll see him sitting. He has a great office, but he's never in it. His determination and boundless passion to serve is how we feed so many people each day." BB pointed to an alcove off the central kitchen. "We're starting lunch prep. No, we don't have downtime between shifts. We just keep rotating."

He led Julie to the area where Dad and Wendy were fixing sandwiches. Two volunteers BB had never met added vegetables to the giant soup kettles. The four fosters sat in their car carriers, blissfully sleeping. Bliss for their foster parents, anyhow.

BB brought Julie up to Dad and Wendy. "Dad, Wendy, meet Julie Williams. Julie, this is my dad and mom, Mick and Wendy Andres."

They shook hands all around. Wendy said, "Welcome. What brings you here?"

Julie dipped her head. "Your son invited me, and I wanted to see what goes on. I've heard about the work the Mission does but have never been before. I'm impressed. And a little overwhelmed." She looked at the assembly line and asked, "What can I do to help?"

Wendy pointed to the heads of lettuce on the counter. "You could break those down into sandwich-size pieces. BB, how about running the slicer and getting us more ham?"

BB grinned at Julie. "And with that, we're off."

She raised her eyebrows but followed Wendy to the lettuce. Dad bumped him in the shoulder. "Nice work bringing another volunteer. Have you known her long?"

BB took his place at the slicing machine. "Just met her. Rescued her from Vic's clutches the other day. Invited her to help serve, and she accepted."

"Promising."

Dad gathered the ham slices and transported them to the sandwich line. When he returned to BB's side, BB shrugged. "I like her. But she's invited me to her dorm room. Twice. I don't know."

Dad's eyes narrowed only a bit. "Did you make it clear why you won't go?"

BB grinned. "You assume I didn't." More ham came off the slicer.

Dad laughed. "I know you better." He motioned to Wendy. "She didn't have a problem with a coed arrangement in the beginning. I was the one who objected. Don't write Julie off just yet."

BB grabbed another hunk of ham and began slicing again. "I'm not. I'm trying to keep it above board. No misunderstandings."

"That's the way to go."

The men went to work in earnest. And the day progressed.

Just after noon, BB looked for Julie. He found her in the office behind DeWayne's desk. He called out to her. "Julie."

She looked up, startled. "BB. I lost you for a few minutes. Thought I'd take a break where no one would see me."

BB extended his hand to her. "Are you ready to go back to the dorms?"

Julie sighed. "I hate to admit I am. I haven't been on my feet this much in a very long time. But I don't want to pull you away from the work."

"I can run you back to the dorm, then return here. It's not a problem."

Julie's eyes sagged, along with the rest of her. "That would be great. We should have come in separate cars." She smiled. "But then I would never know the secret of BB's name."

He pulled her to her feet. "No secret. Just a long story." He led her into the kitchen. "Let me tell Dad and Wendy I'll be back."

He caught Wendy's eye from across the room. She was feeding a baby. From where BB stood, he couldn't guess which one. He motioned to Julie and himself, then pointed to the door. Wendy nodded. BB and Julie walked out the back door and nearly ran over DeWayne. He startled back, nearly dropping an empty tray. He looked up at BB. "Leaving so soon?"

BB laughed. "I've been here since seven-thirty, Pastor. I'm taking Julie back to the dorm. She didn't sign on for the duration."

The pastor shifted the tray to his left hand and held out his right one. "Thank you for coming, Ms. Williams. I appreciate the help. These people appreciate it even more. You don't know what it means to be seen as a person of worth for at least a few hours. It may be the only meal some of our patrons get today unless they can make it back for the next. Some of them may not live that long."

Julie's eyes widened. "That's horrible."

"It's life on the streets. We do what we can while we can." He shook her hand. "Thank you again."

She nodded her head but said nothing else. BB eyed her sideways as they walked back to the car. He held her door open. She slid in. BB closed her door and ran to the other side. He climbed into the car, started the engine, and asked, "Are you okay?"

Julie nodded. "I never thought of it that way. How someone might not make it back for the next meal." She turned to BB. "He knew my name. You introduced me to him once, and he remembered my name. Does he know everyone who comes here? How do you keep track of all these people?"

"We don't. We have to let the Lord bring them around. We pray with the ones who ask and help the ones we can. We supply clothes and sanitary supplies, job information, and counseling services for anyone who wants it. But we can't force anyone to change. They have to want help. Some do. Some just want a warm meal. We won't turn anyone away."

"How many do you serve?"

BB calculated quickly. "Around two hundred each meal."

"And you know who they all are?" Julie chewed on her fingernail.

"No. Oh, I know some of the regulars. Okay, a lot of the regulars. But not nearly all of them." He'd been serving for six months now. Since before the family moved to the new area. Before the fire. Before the wedding. Some things stayed constant. Serving among them.

"So sad." Julie looked out the side window.

BB tried to read what he could see of her face. He wasn't sure what he read there. "Being unhoused is sad. Being hungry is sad. All reasons why we're there."

Julie turned back around. "Who pays for this? It's not tax dollars, I know."

BB hedged. "We have people who give money. And various restaurants donate food items. Leo's Bakery supplies us with day-old bread he can't sell. Some food stores give us the 'ugly' produce they don't want to put on the shelves. We make it enough."

She smiled. A little smile. "You're passionate about this ministry, aren't you?"

He nodded. "Yeah, I am. I'd love to give more hours, but with my school load, I can't. Maybe in the summer."

They arrived at the dorm, and BB walked Julie to the door. She grinned at him. "No sense me inviting you up, is there?"

BB shook his head. "I can't. Won't. Won't put you or myself in a compromising position. It's safer this way."

She "tcked" then said, "A man of morals. I'll talk to you later, BB."

He jumped. "Tonight?"

"I'll have to see." She reached up, kissed him on the cheek, then went into the dorm.

BB rubbed his cheek and sighed. He muttered, "A man of morals. Knight of the Octagon." He turned and walked back to his car. A nudge reminded him, *A child of the King.* "Right. Not a game." He fingered his bracelet, got in the car, and returned to the Mission.

* * *

Ben caught up with Tricia between classes. Alone for once. She scowled at him. "What do you want?"

Ben pulled out the sketch he'd done late the day before. He handed it to her, face down. He shuffled his feet while he waited for her to turn it over and look at it.

Tricia flipped the page over and stared at the drawing. Her eyes narrowed as she looked at it. "That's not me. You didn't draw my braces."

Ben sighed silently. "The braces aren't who you are. They're just something you're wearing."

She snipped, "My clothes are something I'm wearing, and you drew those."

Ben kept from voicing his exasperation but asked, "Do you want me to put the braces in? I can." He held out his hand for the picture.

Tricia pulled it away from him. "No. I'll take it this way." She stared at the sketch for a few moments. "Do I really look like that?"

"Yes." Ben didn't add, *"To me."* Not after the clothes comment. He'd need to think about that one. Maybe telling people he drew them the way he saw them was a bad idea. He'd have to ask Dad. He'd know. He understood about women. Ben had a lot to learn.

Of course, Wendy *was* a woman. Maybe he should ask her. Then he'd really know. Dad would tell him to ask Wendy, anyhow. She was good to have around for more than just feeding the fosters. He needed to help her more. Without grumbling about it. And Jesus would be pleased. He'd start tonight.

A shove from behind threw Ben off balance. He crashed into the locker. Craig laughed, and his voice sounded harsh. "Watch where you're going, punk."

Ben righted himself. A thousand responses flooded his mind. Dad's voice overruled all the mean things he wanted to say. *A gentle answer can prevent fights.*

He straightened his books and moved to go to class.

Craig shoved him again. "I said, watch where you're going, punk."

Ben ignored the bully. He stepped around Craig and went on his way. Anger washed through him. The urge to shove Craig back filled him. But he wouldn't do it. Jesus said to turn the other cheek. Ben would follow Jesus.

Craig grabbed Ben's collar and twirled him around. "Little coward. You won't even fight me."

Students began to chant, "Fight. Fight. Fight." A crowd circled Ben and Craig, their eyes wide. Excited by the prospect of seeing blood, no doubt.

Ben stared at Craig's eyes. He held Craig's gaze. Did he see fear in the bully's eyes? Doubt? Ben stood up a little straighter. He said, "I'm not going to fight you. Jesus would never fight. I won't, either."

The crowd got quiet. Someone taunted, "Ooo, Jesus wouldn't fight. Hit 'im, Craig."

Craig stared at Ben. The voice jeered again, "Hit him. He's a little punk. You're not scared of him, are you? Do it."

Craig huffed. He shouldered his backpack. "He's not worth getting kicked out of school."

An adult voice broke the mood. "Wise choice, Craig. I suggest you boys get to class." Students scattered in every direction. Craig huffed, turned, and walked away. Mr. Hardaway, the principal, nodded to Ben. "That's the way to tackle a bully. Good job, Mr. Andres. I'll let your parents know they can be proud of how you handled yourself."

Ben looked at the ground. He muttered, "I just did what Jesus would do."

Mr. Hardaway laughed. "And you did it very well. Let's get you to class. I'll make sure your teacher doesn't count you late."

Kids watched Ben and Mr. Hardaway walk down the near-empty hall. They probably wondered what Ben had done to get in trouble. Probably thought he was on his way to the principal's office. When Ben turned into his classroom, surprised onlookers pointed and whispered. He smiled to himself. He'd followed Jesus and got rewarded in the end. He'd done it right. He would remember to thank Jesus tonight when he said his prayers.

Of course, he could thank Jesus now. As he took his seat, he prayed, *Thank You, Lord. I didn't want to fight Craig. Will You make him my friend instead of my enemy? In Your Name, amen.* Ben turned his attention to the teacher.

* * *

MONDAY EVENING

BB sat at his desk working on his English paper. Vic, Samuel, and Leeland played cards on Vic's bunk. A knock sounded at the door. Vic yelled, "Come in."

BB scowled. He could only hope it wasn't one of the many girls who presented themselves to the room on all occasions. Mondays were BB's "freedom from distraction" nights when the guys would forgo the parties and the drinking so BB could study. One more of the compromises BB had hammered out.

The door opened, and two uniformed police officers walked in. Samuel, Leeland, and BB came to their feet. Vic continued to lounge on his bunk. One officer chuckled. "At ease, boys. Need to speak to…" he hesitated "…BB?"

BB partially raised his hand. "That would be me. How can I help you?"

Leeland and Samuel returned to sitting on the bunk. BB noted they did not quit paying attention, however.

The lead officer said, "I'm Officer Malone. My partner is Officer Grambling."

BB nodded to both men. "Gentlemen." Officer Grambling looked around the room. He appeared to sniff the air. Looking for something to harass them about? Why were they even here?

Officer Malone led the questioning. He focused all this attention on BB. The police officer didn't even try to look friendly. "Were you at the downtown Mission this week?

"I served there on Friday. I volunteer a couple of times a week." What could this be about? Had something happened?

"It appears someone broke into the donation box and removed a sizable amount of money. Would you know anything about it?" Malone pulled out his note tablet and a pen.

Vic laughed. "Is that where you got the money to pay me? Stealing from the church? Very Christian."

Leeland snapped, "Shut up, Vic. That happened before Friday. Wednesday, in fact."

Officer Malone looked from Vic to BB. "Money?" He made a notation on his pad.

BB frowned. "I pulled money out of my savings on Tuesday to pay off a friend's debt. I have the bank receipt for it."

Malone lifted his chin. "I'll take your word for it. What about Friday? Do you know where the donation box is usually kept?"

BB nodded. He sat back in his chair and motioned for the officers to sit. They declined. BB's gut tightened. "Pastor DeWayne keeps it in the front dining room during the meals. People like to drop in a few cents to a few bucks for their meals. After the last service, Dee puts the box in his office. I was there when he closed for the night, but I can't say I saw the donation box."

BB rolled his pencil between his fingers. "You say a sizable donation. I've never known there to be more than twenty bucks or so in there. How much were they talking about?

Grambling asked, "You count the money, too?"

"Two of us always do. Keeps things honest. I didn't on Friday night, though. I helped Wendy with the fosters."

"The Fosters? Who are they?"

"Foster kids. Foster babies. My folks are taking care of four infants right now. Wendy, my…" Hmm. What relationship did Wendy have to him? Stepmom? Adopted mom? "…my dad's wife was wrestling babies and car seats. I helped her when we closed. Dad must have helped count the money." Why would Pastor Dee call the police for twenty dollars? Why would Dee call the police, period? That's not how they operated.

"Pastor DeWayne said someone put in a check for $20,000. He said it had been put in early in the day. By the time they counted in the evening, it came up missing."

BB's eyes narrowed. He put his pencil down. This was all messed up. How did Pastor Dee know about the check? Did a donor tell him? And why would he leave something so valuable lying around the Mission? Especially leaving the box out where anyone could take it? Things weren't adding up. "I'm confused." Very confused.

Officer Grambling held BB's gaze. "The report said the box had been in the pastor's office. You were seen in the office at noon. No one else remembers the door even being open after then."

This was wrong. Very wrong. BB asked, "Did Pastor Dee file this report himself? Because—"

"We're not concerned with who filed the report. We're concerned about the missing money. You were seen in the office. An office that is always locked, so we were told." The officer's voice hardened.

Vic hooted. "Got you red-handed, dude. Mr. I'm-Better-Than-You."

BB held the officer's eyes and shook his head. "I—" He stopped. Julie had been in the office. An office that Pastor Dee always locked. Would BB implicate her?

He started again. "I need to talk to Pastor DeWayne. Something's not right. I want to call him right now." He reached for his phone, then stopped. "I'm not under arrest or anything, right?"

Grambling sniffed. "Not yet. We came to talk, to find out why you were in a locked office."

BB tapped in the number. Pastor Dee picked up. "BB. What's going on, man?"

"I've got two police officers asking me about a check you reported as missing. Twenty-K worth."

Silence filled the line. "A check for how much?" Incredulity filled the pastor's voice.

"Twenty thousand. Someone filed a police report." BB took it a step further. "They suspect I am involved."

"You? Are we on speaker?"

BB hit the button. "We are now." He swallowed his smile, anticipating what would follow.

Pastor Dee did not disappoint. His voice snapped, "Then listen up. That's the most ridiculous thing I've ever heard. First, I've never seen a check for such an inflated amount at the Mission. I never received one, and I certainly never reported one missing. I don't know who said such a thing, but it's a lie." BB could hear Pastor Dee moving around, shuffling papers. "Bring those police officers to the Mission, and we'll straighten this out. This is outrageous." The volume and tenor of the man's voice rose.

BB raised his eyebrows at the two officers. They looked at each other and then Grambling nodded. BB said, "We'll be down there in twenty minutes." He hung up the phone. "You know where the Mission is?"

Malone nodded. "I've been there a time or two. Pretty nasty area."

"Then you haven't been there lately. Once Pastor Dee got the soup kitchen up and running, it's cleaned up."

Officer Grambling gave BB a jaundiced look. "He some kind of miracle worker?"

BB smiled. "No, but he works for One." BB grabbed his jacket. "Do you want to follow me in my car?"

Officer Malone held up his hand. "Before we do, let me

verify something. What number did you call?" Suspicion laced the man's tone.

"The Mission." BB pulled the phone number up from the internet, showed it to Malone, and then showed him the number he'd just called. They were the same.

Malone humphed. "That's not the number off the report." He pulled it up and showed it to his partner.

Grambling eyed BB, his eyes narrow. "Maybe you better ride in the car with us. So we know you're not running away."

BB exhaled slowly. "I'm not running anywhere. I showed you the number of the Mission. You verified it." He dipped his head. "But I'll ride with you. I'm not afraid."

Vic crowed. "Ooo…he's not afraid. He's got God on his side. Let's see how far God gets you."

Samuel shoved Vic. "Knock it off." He turned his gaze to BB. "If you need a character reference, I'll vouch for you."

Vic sneered, "But who will vouch for you?" He laughed. "If you need a good lawyer, I can recommend one. For a finder's fee, of course." He returned to dealing cards.

BB ignored Vic. His focus remained on the two police officers. "We're going to the Mission, correct?"

"First. Then we'll see where we end up." Grambling kept his eyes on BB.

"Fine." BB walked out of the door to the hallway. Grambling moved ahead of him. Malone took up the rear. BB held his head up. He'd done nothing wrong. He would be vindicated at the Mission.

Scripture again flooded his mind. *When He was accused, He did not answer back but committed Himself to Him Who judges correctly.*

BB would follow Jesus.

They rode in silence to the Mission. BB sat in the back of the cruiser, lifting prayers. He'd done nothing wrong. Should he tell them Julie had been in the office? Or wait until something showed up missing? Maybe wait. See if there would be a need to mention her. Why ruin a good friendship? If they had a good friendship… He hoped they would. Wanted to have one. Wishful thinking on his part? Time would tell.

They parked behind the church and walked into the lighted office. Pastor DeWayne sat at his cluttered desk. Papers lay askew across the bookshelves, on the floor, on the desktop. The office had been trashed. Pastor Dee held a cloth to his forehead. BB jumped when he saw him. "Dee! What happened?" He immediately pulled the cloth away from Pastor Dee's head to reveal a deep cut and a bump the size of a small egg. "Let me get some ice."

He turned away from the police officers and rushed to the kitchen for ice from the freezer. He returned with a bag and a towel and applied it to Dee's head.

Dee explained, "One man. Came in and demanded money. Told him he could have all we'd collected for the day. All five dollars and thirty-one cents of it. He got mad, demanded the checks, and swore we had thousands hidden somewhere. He'd heard on the streets we took in a 20K check just last week. I told him someone lied, and no such check ever came into the Mission during the day." Dee patted his bump and added, "He didn't believe me. Had to check it out for himself."

Grambling and Malone scoured the building. After a few minutes, they returned. Grambling asked, "Did you try to stop him?" The notepad came out.

"No. When he didn't find what he was looking for, he hit me."

BB had a different priority. "Did you lose consciousness?"

"No." Pastor Dee breathed in and out. "I'm fine. I'll be fine." He looked at the police officers. "What's this all about? Who's putting out rumors of us having money? We've never taken in anything more than twenty dollars in a day. That's not how we finance things."

Malone shook his head. "We'll have to find out. You say you didn't file a police report?"

"Never. I'd lose all credibility with my people if I went to the police for something over money. Even this isn't worth reporting." He stopped and added, "Except to the congregation. They'll want to know. They have a right to know."

"You say you never saw a check for twenty thousand dollars?" Grambling couldn't let the issue drop.

"Never in the donation box. And never at this address. If we had, we'd know who it was from, wouldn't we? And we'd simply have them stop the check and issue another."

Officer Malone pulled out his radio and then stopped. "Do you want to file a police report about this?"

Pastor Dee shook his head. He looked at BB and dipped his head to the side. "No. Can't. We operate on a principle of trust. Having a police presence here will nullify all we're trying to do." He eyed the two officers. "Now, if you catch the man who put out the rumors about us having money, we'd be grateful."

"We'll do what we can." Malone turned away from the wounded man and left the building. BB heard the crackle of the radio from the police cruiser.

BB asked, "Doesn't someone who puts in a report have to leave a phone number? Could you do something as simple as call them?"

Officer Grambling's eyes narrowed. He tilted his head to the side. BB could see the wheels turning. After a moment, he pulled up his phone. He typed for a few moments and scrolled for a few more. Finally, he tapped in some numbers.

He put the call on speaker. A crusty voice answered. "Who is this?"

"This is Officer Grambling from the City Police Department. You filed a report with our office—"

The voice snarled. "Knock it off. I know the game. You tell Vic we squared the tables. I made the report. Now, he leaves me alone. We had a deal. He can find someone else to blackmail for his dirty work." The call disconnected.

Those weren't the exact words the voice used, but BB translated them through the Holy Spirit to keep them clean.

Grambling pulled the phone away to look at it as if to see the speaker. The officer stared at BB as he put the phone back in its place. "Vic? Does the name mean anything to you?"

Rage built in BB's gut. Dee was attacked because of Vic's little stunt. And for what? Why would he even arrange something like this?

Did the why matter? Vic's actions jeopardized the Mission and everyone around it. Is that what he intended?

BB clenched his fists. "Yeah. He's my roommate. Vic Shields."

"You know anything else about this you want to tell me?"

BB shook his head. His voice shook. "I have no idea. I don't know anything. Except he got a friend hurt."

Dee patted BB's arm. "Tried to get a friend hurt. Can't hurt me by hitting me in the head. Too tough."

BB gritted his teeth. "This isn't a joke."

Dee snapped back, "Make it one." He moderated his tone. "Let it go, BB. We know where the rumor came from, and we can counter it. There won't be any more trouble, I promise."

Officer Grambling nodded to Dee. "We'll talk to Mr. Shields all the same. Filing a false report is something we take seriously." He looked at BB. "We should take you back to campus. And apologize for the inconvenience."

BB breathed out slowly. "Not your fault." Blame lay squarely with Vic. The only question was why. Not that BB cared. There could be no excuse.

The ride to the dorm proved to be as quiet as the ride to

the Mission had been. Lots of time for tension to build. Voices in his head to repeat accusations over and over. Anger to go from simmering to full boil. Blood pressure to rise. Muscles to tense and come on alert.

BB stomped from the cruiser to the dorm entrance. The two police officers followed him. As they rode the elevator to the fifth floor, Officer Grambling warned, "Battery gets you a weekend in jail. It won't look good on your school record. Or your police record."

BB let the words of wisdom wash over him. He didn't care. He didn't. Vic had hurt a friend and tried to destroy the Mission's credibility. Dee would heal, but what about the Mission? Vic deserved a beatdown for what he'd done. But no, the punk would walk like he always did.

Punk wasn't the word BB preferred. No, he wanted to use something stronger. Something that expressed the depth of his hatred. His disgust. His self-righteous—

A vision of the crucified Christ slipped into his mind. BB wanted to push it out, to remember instead the lump on Pastor Dee's head. But the vision wouldn't go away. It stared at BB from the cross.

The elevator doors opened. BB strode toward the room. Grambling stepped in front of BB, cutting him off from any unlawful action. Like attacking Vic. Which BB sorely wanted to do.

Samuel and Vic sat at Vic's desk watching a video. As soon as Vic saw the police, he closed the laptop and turned to face the newcomers.

"Well, well. Look what the cat drug in. Why are you back here? I thought you were going to jail."

Grambling took Vic by the arm. "No, but you are."

Vic's eyes widened, and his jaw dropped open. Grambling pulled him to his feet by his arm. Vic bellowed, "What? What are you talking about?"

"You're under arrest for filing a false police report."

"You can't do that! I didn't do anything. I'll have your

badge."

"If you can get it, you can have it." Grambling did not sound intimidated.

Vic's protests accelerated as the officer herded him out of the door. Samuel and Leeland watched as the officers escorted Vic down the hall. As the voices faded, BB sank on Leeland's bunk. He stared at his fists. Shame washed over him.

Leeland crowed, "Finally!"

Samuel stared at BB. "What just happened? What's going on?" The lineman stood in front of BB, his hands on his hips.

BB looked up. Depression swamped him. "Vic had someone file the report about the check being stolen. Because of the filing, a rumor got out the Mission had money. Someone broke in and beat Pastor Dee in the head, trying to steal it." BB opened his hands and examined his palms. "I wanted to whip him. I wanted to beat him to a pulp. I wanted to take revenge and deal vengeance." His voice choked. "I wanted to do everything I know I should never do." Tears welled in his eyes. "I denied the Lord. I didn't care what He wanted."

Samuel relaxed and shrugged. "Eh. You're human. I wasn't sure. Now I am."

Leeland asked, "What's going to happen to Vic?"

BB shook his head. "Probably nothing. His father will get him off like always."

Samuel stretched and picked up his laptop. "Maybe. To hear Vic talk, he and his folks are anything but tight these days." Samuel put his computer away on his desk, then turned to BB. "Don't feel bad. You'll be a hero for putting him in his place."

A hero to who? He hadn't done anything. The police took Vic down. BB had been there when it happened. He wouldn't take credit.

Nor blame. BB pulled off his shoes, changed into his

sweats, and climbed onto his bunk. Sleep would come after prayers. *Forgive me, Lord. And be with Vic. Reach his heart, Father. Please.*

* * *

TUESDAY

Well?
Done. No more problem.
We'll see.
Let me know.

Vic showed up the next morning to shower, get dressed, and head to class. Samuel caught the man by his arm. "So what happened?"

Vic shrugged. "My dad had to straighten out the little mix-up." He glared at BB. "That you tried to pin on me."

BB pulled his books together. "I pinned nothing on you. The police did all the calling."

"Yeah, that's what they said. I'll believe it when you're the one behind bars. You think you're untouchable because you're so holy. We'll see how holy you are when—"

Samuel caught Vic's arm. "Come on, man. We've got class. And better things to do than beat a dead horse. Let's go."

"Dead horse is right. You're dead meat, Andres." Vic stormed out of the room with Samuel behind him.

Leeland, who'd been staying low in his bunk, looked out at BB. "Dude scares me."

BB raised his eyebrows. "Don't let him get to you. Take nothing from him, and he can't do anything. He's a lot of mouth."

"Yeah, and his dad gets him off every time."

"Maybe." Scripture crossed his mind. *God knows how to preserve the wicked against the day of judgment.*

Pray for your enemies.

No conflict. God's job, BB's job. He lifted a, *Help him, Lord,* and headed to class. His phone pinged. He checked the message as he crossed the commons.

Julie. He tagged her back. *What's up?*

You free tonight?

Yes.

Dinner? Café Dinero?

Time?

Six?

Pick you up or meet you there?

Pick me up. Save parking.

BB grinned. *See you at six outside the dorm.*

See you.

BB resisted the urge to add "KO." It would bring up too many questions. Questions he wasn't sure he wanted to answer.

But he did have a question for Julie. What had she been doing in the office at the Mission, and how had she gained access? Sure, she said she wanted to take a break. But Pastor Dee always locked the office. Did she have anything to do with Vic's rumors?

He wanted to believe she didn't. Wanted to believe she genuinely cared about him as a person. But he wanted to believe in Santa Claus, too, and he knew how far that took him.

He shuffled off to class.

BB saw Riley Crimmons headed toward him. He scowled, then arranged his countenance in a friendlier manner. Don't start with a fight. Be kind. Be smart.

Riley and her entourage of three other young women, all bright and beautiful, stopped in front of him. The paisley dress she wore was too tight in some places, too open in others. Meant to entice. She placed her books on her hip and gave him a look of pure concern. "I'm so sorry about your pastor. Did he get hurt badly?"

"No, thank the Lord. Bump on his head, but otherwise he's fine." *How does she know about the break-in?*

Riley nodded. "That's good. What's this I hear about the Mission having thousands of dollars stolen? Your homeless population must be doing very well if they can donate that kind of change."

BB breathed slowly in and out before answering. "It was a lie. We never had a check for that amount. Or any amount. Our people don't use checks." *They barely use money at all.*

Riley's jaw dropped open in an exaggerated look of surprise. "You mean someone *lied* about a check? Why would anyone do such a thing?"

BB kept his tone even. Or as even as possible. "I don't know. Only the person who started the rumor knows."

Riley put a finger on her chin. "It must have been someone who had a grudge. They must have had something against someone at the Mission."

BB's gut tightened. "It could be. I'm certain the police would be interested in your theory."

Riley's eyes widened in mock surprise. "But I heard the Mission wasn't pursuing prosecution. Something about ruining the reputation of the church? How are the police involved?"

"Someone filed a false police report and implicated Vic. That makes it police business. The authorities take filing bogus claims very seriously."

Riley arched her brows. She shifted her weight to stare BB in the face. "As seriously as ignoring a summons?"

What was she driving at? He paused. "Probably. Maybe more. I don't know. I'm not a lawyer." He smiled to try to take some of the chill from the air. "I'm studying physics, not law."

Riley did not respond to the attempt at de-escalation. "Most people on campus recognize when I invite them to a party, it's a summons. And missing a summons is serious business."

BB groaned inwardly. He kept his smile and his temper. "I'm sorry I didn't recognize the gravity of the invitation. But I'd still have to decline. I'm not a party person, Riley. Never have been, never will be."

"I can be the judge of that. You'd be a perfect match for my friends. I would introduce you to all the best people. I've already got a list started." Her eyes narrowed. "Don't turn me down twice."

BB dodged. "Do you have liquor at your parties?"

"Of course. It's required. What kind of host would I be if I denied my guests the ability to imbibe their favorite beverages?"

"I don't drink liquor, Riley. I'm not a teetotaler, but I don't drink liquor. I'm underage."

Riley shrugged. "So? There's no problem. You can still attend, escort my friends, and not drink. You'll find the party far more enjoyable if you do loosen up, of course. No one likes a stick-in-the-mud escort." She smiled. "Of course, we supply more than alcohol to help you relax."

BB shook his head. Time to make the stand. "Riley, I follow Jesus as my Lord and Savior. What you're talking about is in direct opposition to His will for my life." He held her eyes. "I'm not speaking for anyone else but myself. For me, it's a no. I can't attend your parties."

Riley's face hardened. "You're refusing my summons, then?"

BB nodded. "Yes, I am."

Riley held his eyes. "Others thought they could refuse me, too." She brushed past him. "We'll see how you fare compared to them."

BB waited until the posse passed him, then shook his

head. He was worried about his roommates, and now this? He murmured, "Lord, keep me in the center of Your will. Guard my back, my front, and every side of me. Please. As You will, Father. In Jesus' Name, amen." He continued to class.

* * *

TUESDAY AFTER SCHOOL

Ben sat on the floor, surrounded by the babies. Tricia sat with him. She rocked Sassy in her arms, crooning softly to the infant. Her face was lit up with a glow that cast shadows across her features. Ben liked light and shadow. It gave depth to Tricia's face. She'd agreed to come over after school to meet the babies and maybe look at some of his other drawings. Her mother, who she lived with now, didn't mind. At least she knew where Tricia would be after school.

Tricia placed Sassy back in the middle of the baby pile. "You're so lucky. You've got a mom, a dad, a brother, and all these babies. I got nothing." She sighed from the bottom of her feet.

Ben tried to encourage her. "You've got your dad and your mom."

"But they're not together. They don't even talk to each other." Again, the sigh.

Ben looked at the floor. He cleared his throat. "You've got friends. I see you with them all the time at school." Tricia usually had a posse of four or five girls with her.

Tricia snorted and tossed her head. "That bunch. They only follow me because they think they'll get boys that way." She glared at Ben. "Boys only follow me because they think they can get my attention. And not in a good way."

Ben raised his eyes. "I wanted your attention. But to be a friend." He hoped it sounded okay.

She nodded. "I know. You're different from the others."

Ben lowered his head. "I know. I'm always different." The uncomfortable feeling in his stomach started. Different usually meant something bad.

Tricia jumped. "Not like that, Ben. I mean, you're different in a good way. You treat me like a person, not like something you can use." She touched his hand. "I like you."

His hand tingled. Ben looked into Tricia's eyes. He liked the way they shone in the light. "I like you, Tricia." Should he have said that?

Wendy walked into the room. "Do you two want drinks? I've got soft drinks or lemonade." She smiled. "I even have water."

Tricia pulled her hand back sharply. "Lemonade would be wonderful, Mrs. Andres."

"One lemonade. Ben?"

Ben climbed to his feet. "I'll get the drinks." He needed to think. Was he doing the right thing? Should they touch hands? Would Jesus do such a thing?

Wendy waved him down. "I'll get them. You stay with your guest."

Ben sat back down. He picked up Chris and bounced the baby on his shoulder. Was it okay to touch hands with Tricia? Maybe even hold hands? He needed to talk to Dad. Tricia said she liked him. He liked her, too. Did that mean it was okay?

Wendy came back with the drinks and placed them on the coffee table. "Safer here. No babies rolling into them."

Ben settled Chris in his lap so the baby could look around rather than stare at the ceiling. Tricia laughed. "I bet they get tired of looking up all the time."

"It's better than being on their tummies looking at the blanket." Should he have touched hands with Tricia?

Tricia cooed over the babies. "They're so sweet. Don't

you wish you could adopt all of them?" She wiggled Aldi's feet. The infant rolled over and giggled.

Ben nodded. "We might if no one else wants them."

Tricia's face lit up. "Really? You'd take them all?"

"Yeah, I mean, if no one else does. Dad and Wendy don't want to see the babies go into regular foster care, where they could be bounced around from place to place. We have a big house. We could take them in."

"But how would you feel about having all these babies to take care of? Doesn't it get tiring?"

Ben leaned over to whisper in Tricia's ear. "It does." He sat back and added, "But Jesus wants us to care for orphans, so we would do it. And Dad makes sure I don't have to stay with them all the time. I have other things I do, too."

"Yeah? Like what?" Tricia challenged him.

"I go to art class. I have art at school, too, but I'm taking classes at the community center. And I play basketball at the Mission when Dad and Wendy are helping fix meals."

"I'm jealous. You guys are always doing something." Tricia sat with her legs tucked into her. She wrapped her arms around her knees.

Ben thought. Hard. "Would you like to come to church with us?"

Tricia shook her head. "Church is boring. All they do is sit and sing songs I can't understand. The pastor stands behind this box and tells us everything we're not supposed to do. I don't like it."

Ben leaned back against the couch. "No wonder you don't like it. I wouldn't like it, either. Our church isn't like that at all. We stand when we sing, and we clap and raise our hands. And the pastor tells jokes and walks up and down the stage. He talks to the people in the seats. And when I'm not in the main service, I help with the preschool class." He made Chris wave his little hand. "Come with us. You'll see. It's different."

Tricia dipped her head to the side. "I'll think about it.

You want me to come this weekend?"

"If you can." Ben stopped. "I mean, if you want to. We come back here and have lunch after. You're welcome to come then, too. Stay as long as you want. Dad can take you home whenever you decide it's time to leave, or when your mom says you have to come home.

Tricia patted Sassy's back. "I'll think about it. I'll tell you at school tomorrow."

Ben beamed. "That would be great."

Tricia looked at Ben sideways. "No one's ever invited me to church before. I get asked to dances and the movies and stuff but never to church. That will be different."

Ben considered it a moment. "I guess my family is different, too."

"But in a good way." She beamed at him and touched his hand again.

Ben smiled. "Yeah. Sometimes it's good to be different." Not always. Just sometimes. Like now.

* * *

BB came back to the room before his date to dump off his books. Vic sat on his bunk, staring at the floor, his hands on his knees. He looked up at BB as he came in. BB dropped his book on his desk and faced the man. "Vic, I didn't—"

"I know. You didn't have anything to do with last night. They told me. I believe you. My dad cleared up the problem. We're cool. It's all good."

BB wanted to squint, to narrow his eyes and question this sudden change of tone. But he resolved not to react. "Thanks." But he had to ask. "What happened?"

"Turns out someone threw out my name to get me in trouble. Not related to you at all. Once the cops figured out I had been set up, they let me go. Of course, my dad had to get involved and connect the dots for them. Didn't take long after that."

"I'm glad." How could BB lie with a straight face? *Sorry, Lord. I will be glad once this is all over.* "You been to class today?"

"Nah, I took a mental health day. Trauma and all. I've got better things to do. Coach wants another practice tonight under the lights. Get us ready for prime time."

BB lifted his head. "I see. How many games do you have at night?"

"Two right now. The TV networks haven't decided on two others. But Coach wants us ready. This is the year we go to conference finals."

BB held out his fist. "Do it."

Vic tapped his knuckles with BB. "You know it."

BB changed into a clean shirt while Vic stretched out on his bunk. BB snuck several looks at his roommate. This seemed too different for the man. BB didn't trust it. *Lord, forgive me, but his attitude is strange. You can work miracles, but my gut says this isn't one of them. This is something else.*

BB polished his image in the mirror and set out the door. He called, "I'll see you later tonight."

Vic thumped the bottom of the bed above him. "You going out with Julie?"

"Just dinner. She invited me."

"Nice when they initiate for a change."

BB grinned and leaned against the door. "Don't I know it." He took one last look at Vic and said, "Nite, man."

"Yeah."

BB shook his head, walked to the parking lot, climbed in his car, and drove to Julie's dorm. He waited five minutes for her to come down. She breezed past him. "You can come up, you know."

"Nope. Can't do it."

"It's a co-ed dorm. You can hang outside the door if you're squeamish."

They walked to BB's car. "Trying to respect the boundaries." He opened the door for Julie, then closed it behind her. BB slid around, jumped in his side of the car, and started the motor.

"Even when I don't have the same ones you do?" Julie smiled at him. Demure smile.

"Especially then." BB shuddered. She laughed and put her hand on his neck. BB put the car in gear and headed out.

They drove the twenty minutes to the restaurant. BB watched the road but asked, "How are your classes going?"

"Advanced Algebra is the pits."

BB laughed. "English isn't much better. I swear it's my first language, but I'm beginning to wonder if I speak it at all. I thought I only had to worry about present and past tenses. Now, there's a whole world of them."

"I know what you mean. I used to love numbers. Now, not so much. Imaginary numbers cross the line." Julie scowled.

Talking about numbers could be safe. He'd do that. "Right. A real-world application would be nice. Something I can see and understand." *I can trust You with what I can't see, but imaginary numbers are a step too far. I get it, but I don't.*

"Not in our first year, I don't think. That may be for advanced study. Second or third year only." Julie kneaded the back of his neck. While it felt good, it also made him uncomfortable. Why did he have to have such mixed feelings?

The drive flew by. BB found a parking space near the door of the establishment. The lot looked only half-full. Not bad for a school night.

Julie climbed out without waiting for BB to open her door. She waited for him to close it, however. He looked at the sign and asked, "How's the food?"

She smiled and tapped his cheek. "I come for the scenery."

BB fell in step behind her and shook his head. *En garde.* He would have to watch his step. And hers.

They got a table near the back but away from the

kitchen. The lighting seemed bright enough to study. A few tables hosted students buried in their books. The restaurant provided a quiet place away from the dorms and the library. Any port in a storm, it seemed.

Julie ordered a crispy chicken salad. BB ordered four street tacos. Both appeared after only minutes and looked fit to eat. BB hesitated, then asked, "May I bless the food?"

Julie's eyes sparkled. "If you think it needs it."

BB nodded. "Always."

"Be my guest." Julie waved her hand, then laid it on the table.

BB took Julie's hand, bowed his head, and prayed quietly, "Thank You, Father, for this time together. Bless our thoughts, our words, and our food. In Your Name, I ask all things, amen."

Julie looked up. "Very nice."

BB swallowed his first bite, then asked, "What did you think of the Mission?"

Julie looked off to the side. "I still can't get past the thought some of those people might not live to come back for their next meal. That doesn't really happen, does it? Not every day."

"No, not every day. But it happens. Living on the streets can be deadly."

"Then why do people choose to live like that?"

"Not everyone chooses to be unhoused." BB chewed his taco. "We don't get into the 'why' of people as much as what can we do to help them off the streets? We've got resources all across town to help if people want it."

"Why wouldn't they?"

BB shrugged. "Lots of reasons. Some have pets, and shelters won't take animals. Some don't want to give up their drug habit. Don't want to follow the rules. Don't like being told what to do and how to do it. It's self-destructive, but people have reasons. We don't judge. We provide a hot meal and a place to get clean. Showers and washer and dryer."

"And it's all free." Julie eyed him sideways.

"Free to those who need it. Or want it. Again, we don't judge. We serve."

"But who pays for it? Where does the money come from?" Julie poked around in her salad. She stabbed a piece of chicken and chewed on it.

BB breathed as Popdad Quinn taught him. "We have corporate and private donors who fund it." He turned the conversation. "We appreciated the extra hands. I'm sorry we wore you out." BB asked, "How'd you get into the office? It's usually always locked."

Julie shrugged this time. "It was open. I was looking for an out-of-the-way place to sit where I wouldn't be caught lounging. The office seemed like the perfect place."

"Hmm." Something didn't ring true. The office had been closed when he'd gone by at eleven. Pastor Dee never left it unlocked. Never.

But he had no proof of anything, either. He asked, "Do you think you'll return and serve again?"

Julie hesitated. "I don't know. It's pretty intense. And I don't have lots of free hours. I'll see what my schedule looks like." She savored another piece of spicy chicken, then set her fork down. "I heard you paid off Leeland's debt to Vic. How'd you do it?"

"I drew money out of my savings." Why the question?

"I see. That explains it."

"Explains what?" BB leaned in closer.

Julie tossed her head. "The dead body they found? Word has it he'd been a drug dealer. Someone knocked him off for his territory. Then you show up the next day with six bills to pay off Leeland's debt. Rumors got started."

Flames burned in BB's gut. And they weren't from the tacos. "Someone is spreading rumors I killed a drug dealer, and that's how I got the money? Is that what you're saying?"

Julie held up her hand. "Don't get upset. I told you it's just a rumor. You know how things get tossed around." She stabbed the lettuce in her salad.

Quinn's voice filled his head. Breathe. Do not let them see you react. You do, they have more ammunition. Breathe, smile, and say, 'That's interesting.' And leave it go.

BB breathed out slowly. "That's interesting." He cocked his head. Something wasn't adding up. "How do you know Leeland? And who told you about the arrangement?"

Julie flipped a curl behind her shoulder. "He sat there the time Vic crowded me. And I threatened Mr. Shields with my taser." Again, she concentrated on her salad.

"No one introduced you two," BB probed.

Julie held BB's eyes. "What are you saying? I caught it in conversation."

"That doesn't explain how you knew about the payoff."

Julie's eyes narrowed. "What is this, an interrogation? I heard about it, okay? What does it matter where or who?" Anger laced her tone.

BB backed off slightly. "Because I like to know who started the rumor so I can correct it. And stop lies from spreading."

His date attacked her salad. She ate another two forkfuls, then sniffed. "It's true you paid off Leeland's debt. And flashed six bills to do it. It's not all rumor."

"And I have the receipt where I took the money from my bank. Should I post it for everyone to see? On the community billboard?"

Julie laid her fork down. "I'm not trying to get you upset, BB. I wanted to know the truth behind the rumor, that's all. I didn't figure you for the drug dealer type."

"Thanks." He kept the sarcasm from his tone. Or most of it, anyhow. "I wanted to help Leeland get out from under Vic." This was not at all how he'd imagined the date would go.

"Like you want to help the people at the Mission. I get it."

"Right." BB finished his tacos. Time to change the

subject. He needed to think. "You want some churros for dessert?"

Julie grinned. "They have a *tres leches* cake that is to die for."

BB held up his hand to draw the waiter's attention and ordered the desserts.

The cake was as delicious as Julie promised. BB paid for dinner, and Julie got the tip. BB watched to make sure she left a decent one. He would have found a way to supplement it if she hadn't. She did. He could leave with a clear conscience.

They left the café and wandered around the small sidewalk mall, looking in the windows. BB reached out and took Julie's hand. She smiled at him. They strolled the walk for fifteen minutes before it became clear they'd seen all there was to see. Tobacco shop. Dry Cleaners. Nail Salon. Half-price book store. Nothing held BB's interest. Julie seemed content to walk. They reached the end of the strip, turned around, and walked back. BB held the door open to his car and waited for Julie to climb in. She grinned at him. "Remember, only when I get in. I can open it myself on the way out."

BB laughed. "I know. I know. I'm trying to make my dad proud of me." *And the Lord. But you don't mention Him, do you, Julie?* "He wanted to rear a proper gentleman."

"Oh, he did. Maybe too much. You can come to my room, and we won't do anything untoward. Just hang out."

"We could. But why take the chance? Why put us in a position where people will talk? More than they're talking now." He needed to find out how far the rumors of him dealing drugs had spread. And what he should do about it. If it had been just Vic, he could stop him. If it had gone further…he would have to face it when it came. If it came. *Lord, I know You will uphold my honor. Or You won't, and I'll learn from it. But if I have a choice, please protect my reputation.*

They drove back to the dorms. BB parked in front of Julie's. He stayed behind the steering wheel and held her hand. "Thank you for tonight. I had a good time."

Julie smiled. Her eyes glowed. "I did, too. And I'll ask again. Will you come up? I'm sure my roommates are there. We'll be chaperoned."

BB shook his head. But he leaned in for a goodbye kiss. A sweet, gentle, quiet kiss.

Julie kissed him back. And it wasn't gentle, and it wasn't quiet. But it was sweet. She leaned in for a second kiss, but BB pulled back. He cleared his throat. "Um, that better be it. For now. Thank you, Julie." Time for him to go. Now. Before he felt something he didn't want to feel.

She put her hand behind his head and tried to pull him to her. BB pulled back, not with force, but with resolution. "No. Call it a night. I'll see you again soon." He asked, "Sunday for church?"

Julie's face lost half its glow. She shrugged. "I'll let you know." She slid out of the car but leaned over before exiting. "You are the most exasperating man I've met. I'm not sure I can survive your morals."

BB sighed. "I'd say I'm sorry, but I'm not. I can't be. You're special, Julie. But special isn't enough to compromise what I believe. I will hold to it."

"Your reputation." A note of sarcasm laced her response.

He corrected, "My Lord."

"Right." Julie shook her head, stood, and closed the door. She did not look back as she walked into the dorm building.

BB watched her disappear then sighed. "Why's this got to be so difficult?"

He knew why. He adjusted his bracelet on his wrist and headed over to his dorm. Maybe he'd catch a break, and no one would be there. Or Vic would be mellowed out and wouldn't make trouble.

His phone pinged. He looked at the text. Pastor Dee. *Need you to come by the Mission as soon as you're able.*

BB looked at the time. Just before nine. If Pastor Dee texted him, chances were good Dee was still at the Mission himself. BB had a full class load tomorrow. He texted back, *Tonight or Thursday.*

Tonight. See you when you get here.

KO

What could be so important? Had there been more trouble from the supposed donations? Had someone else accused the Mission of having money? Had there been another break-in? A hundred scenarios ran through his head as he drove to the downtown location.

Lights were still on in the front and the office of the church. BB parked around back as always and spotted a familiar car. What would Dad be doing here?

He walked into the office to find Pastor Dee sitting behind his desk. Dad sat in a folding chair to the side. His elbows rested on his knees. His head rested on his folded hands. BB's insides twisted. Something was wrong with all this. Something bad wrong.

Pastor DeWayne motioned for BB to take a chair in front of the desk. Papers had been cleared and the desk looked like someone actually worked there. Children's coloring sheets of Jesus and the woman at the well hung from the chalkboard behind Dee. A wealth of books graced the far wall. Everything in its place. So, this wasn't about a break-in. Good. Cancel that worry.

BB tapped his knuckles with his dad. He tried to smile around the tightness in his chest. "What's going on, Pastor?" He looked at his dad. "What got you out this late?" He sat in the chair Dee indicated.

Pastor Dee cleared his throat. "I wanted your dad here when I talked to you." The man hesitated, then seemed to push forward. "Word from the street has reached us you're dealing drugs."

He let the accusation sink in. Then continued, "We know it's a lie. No one on the staff believes it. No one who knows you believes it."

BB looked at his dad. "Dad?" His voice cracked. So did his heart.

Dad came out of his seat and put his arm on BB's shoulder. "We know there's no truth in the rumors. None. I know you. You love the Lord too much to turn on Him like that." He snorted. "And there's no need. Your inheritance from your Popdad is enough to last you ten lifetimes. You don't need money. Ever." Dad looked at Pastor Dee. "But what do we do?"

BB's insides crumbled. If the rumor had reached Pastor Dee…if it truly had reached the street…

Then BB's reputation was finished. Only those who knew him would believe in him. And even they might wonder. In the back of their minds, they would still question...

Hollow. Everything in him hollowed out. "How? How did this reach you? I haven't heard anything about it."

Pastor Dee held BB's eyes steady. "Gee's daughter works at the campus. In the cafeteria. She heard some female students discussing the death that was reported on Saturday. The police first thought it was suicide. They'd found a note. But they began investigating further, so the girls said, and now think it was murder. Your name came up. You were flashing money around like it was water."

Dee laid his hand on his desk. "The women were texting all their friends to watch out for BB. Sharing a picture of you on socials. Gee's daughter told them she knew you, and you would never be involved in something like that. You volunteer at the Mission and are a good man. One of the women threatened her. Told her she better keep her mouth shut about her opinions, or she'd be implicated, too. She was pushing everyone to warn their friends about what a danger you are on campus. That's how I heard it."

BB looked at his dad. "What do I do? How do I stop this?" Water burned his eyes. "Even if the one who started the rumor were to stand in front of the student body and say it wasn't true, it would still be out there." He stared at Pastor Dee. "And if you heard it, the rumor might have beyond the school. Anyone could know about it with social media. Where else?" His jaw went slack. "Dad?" He sagged in his chair. "I did a good thing. I paid off Leeland's debt. And now I'm getting crucified for it."

He bowed his head and closed his eyes. Dad squeezed his shoulder. BB heard him pray in anguish, "Lord, my son is hurting. I'm hurting. I want to punch out whoever started this rumor. It's a lie. It's a lie, and whoever they are, they know it's a lie. This is malicious and cruel and wrong. What do we do? How do we right the wrong? How do we restore BB's reputation?"

Dad paused, then continued, his voice broken. "But You know what it is to be wrongly accused. You did nothing but heal and love and forgive, and they crucified You. You know what this is. I know You can make something out of this. You have a plan and a purpose. But can You show it to us? Show it to BB? Help him understand what You expect of him. Of all of us. Oh, Lord, help us."

BB wanted to squirm. It wasn't his dad's reputation that had been shot. It was BB's.

Or maybe his dad had been affected. Would this keep them from being foster parents? Would it reflect on Ben? How far would it go?

He closed his eyes. Lord, please. Make it stop. Right this wrong.

Scripture whispered in his ear. If anyone wants to be My servant, let him deny himself, take up his cross, and follow Me.

BB went still inside. So far, following Jesus had cost him nothing. Not personally. Oh, there had been the crazies who wanted to kill him and his family and all the Knights, but it had been greed, not persecution. This…this…

This was an attack on him for his love of the Lord. There would be no other reason to go after him like this.

BB opened his eyes and looked at Pastor Dee. His voice sounded calm, even to his ears. "I know what this is. It's a personal attack on my faith. And the enemy will not win."

Dad squeezed BB's shoulder again and gave BB a straight-lipped smile. "Good man." He returned to his chair, looked at Dee, and asked, "What do we do?"

Dee shook his head. "We do nothing different. You're still a volunteer here." He smiled without mirth. "If people believe you're dealing, they will have to get over it."

BB lowered his head. "Are you sure you don't want me to stop?" BB's voice cracked again.

Pastor Dee's held heat. "No. Absolutely not. If you don't show up like normal, it will be an admission you've done something wrong. It will be proof they were right. But if you keep working, people will see we have faith in you and will get over the rumors faster."

BB lifted his eyes to meet Dee's. "You honestly believe that?"

"Of course I do. It's what I expect from this group. If anyone says anything different, you refer them to me." Dee nodded firmly. And pounded his fist on his desk.

BB looked at his dad. "Does this affect you and the foster program?" The possibility crushed him.

Dee added his inquiry. "Will this impact your ability to take in foster babies, Mick?"

Dad raised his eyebrows. "It might. We'll cross that bridge when we come to it. If they believe we're unfit, they could take the babies away." He shrugged and turned to BB. "The fact you're not living at home may make a difference. We'll see."

Dad sounded confident. BB knew better. His voice reflected how broken he felt. "Does that mean I can't come home? Or shouldn't?"

There was anger in Dad's voice. He snapped, "No, it does not. You're my son. It's your home, too. You remember that. Never think for one minute you're not welcome or part of the family."

"What about Ben? What will happen to him?" BB continued to imagine the devastation this rumor would cause. "He'll be painted with the same brush...ostracized because of me." How would Ben handle it? His first year in public school, and now his brother is accused of being a drug dealer?

He needed to call Julie. He needed to find out who started this. Vic had to be behind it. Could this be revenge for paying off Leeland's debt? Or just because Vic hated BB? He mocked BB all the time for believing in Christ.

He missed what Dee had said. "...we go before the congregation on Sunday to combat this." Pastor's eyes narrowed. "You up to it? You gonna be here Friday and show the ones who question you what a man is made of?"

BB nodded. He straightened his shoulders and sat up tall. "I am. I will. This won't beat me."

Dad shoved him lightly. "Of course, it won't. I'll have the Knights praying for you. And out there countering the lies."

"Do they know about it?" How could word have reached his friends and family when he had only learned about it now?

"Rumor mills thrive on social media. Kay monitors most of the feeds for our group. If she saw anything, she'd be on it. But even she shuts down for the night. The rest of the Knights will know about it in the morning."

Truth. BB relaxed only slightly. "Right." He looked from his dad to Pastor Dee. "I should go back to the dorm. I'll be here first thing Friday morning."

Dee asked, "Are you in shape to go back? In control? Calm? Centered on Jesus?"

BB exhaled. "Yes." He looked at his lap. "I went out

with Julie this evening. She asked me about the rumor. Wouldn't say where she heard it, but she knew about my paying off Leeland's debt." He looked up. "I need to talk to her and find out where she heard this. Maybe I can find the source."

Dee's voice sounded gentle. "And then what? You said it yourself. Even if he stood on the clock tower and announced to the world he lied, there would be those who wouldn't believe him. They'll believe the lie but not the truth because the lie is more dramatic. More interesting. More fun to believe."

BB dropped his eyes. "I still need to know who my enemy is."

Dee quoted, "'We don't fight against flesh and blood, but against—'"

"I know, Pastor. But I need to know who my earthly enemy is. If only so I don't give him any more ammunition." BB stood up. He extended his hand. "Thanks, Brother Dee."

The pastor came out from behind his desk and gave BB a strong hug. "The Lord is my rock and my fortress. The Lord is a strong tower."

BB smiled. "My house is built on the Rock. I won't crumble."

Dad hugged him. "You can stay at home tonight if you want."

BB shook his head. "No, I've got to face the lion sooner or later." He held his dad's eyes. "I'm sorry, Dad."

Dad rattled BB's shoulders hard. "Do not say that. Ever. This is not your fault. We always knew persecution would come. We've faced it in small ways. Now, we face it together." He cupped his hand behind BB's neck. "Love you, son."

BB hugged his dad. "Love you, Dad." He drew in a deep breath and turned to leave. He turned back. "Tell Ben I'll see him this weekend."

"I'll pass him the message."

BB walked out of the office and the building. He climbed into his car and then pulled out his phone. He stared at the time. After eleven. Would Julie still be up? Should he talk to her or let it go?

He needed to know. He texted, *You up?*

Still. What's up?

Need to talk.

Tomorrow.

Classes tomorrow. Tonight?

Subject?

Rumors. Reached my dad and Pastor. Need to know where you heard it.

There was a long silence. Finally, she responded, *Friday. I'll meet you at the Mission. We can talk there.*

BB stared at the screen. It would be the best he could hope for. *See you there.* He started the car. "Lord, direct my steps. Lead me. This hurts. But remind me, You hurt, too. If I've done anything to add to this, forgive me. I know what You did. Show me what You want me to do. Always. And especially now. In the Name of Your Son, Jesus. Amen."

He put the car in drive and headed back to the dorm.

* * *

THURSDAY

Ben slashed black paint across the page on his desk. It matched his mood. Dark. Black. Someone accused his brother of dealing drugs. His brother. BB. BB would never deal drugs. Never. Uncle Petey dealt drugs and got killed for it. BB knew better. He would never, ever sell drugs.

But someone had started a rumor, and now people believed it. People who didn't even know his brother.

He swiped two more black strokes across the page.

Mrs. Wellford asked, "Is this the start of a night sky, Ben?"

Ben sighed. "No." He completed the darkness.

Mrs. Wellford's tone came out gentle. "Who are you mad at?"

Ben lowered his head. "The people who hurt my brother." He looked up, and tears stung his eyes. "They're lying about him and saying he's selling drugs. My brother would never sell drugs. Ever." Anger made his words sharp.

Mrs. Wellford nodded. "I know, Ben. Your brother is a good man. It's awful someone would lie about him. But he'll come through this. I'm sure he will. And he'll be stronger for having done it. You mustn't let this drag you down as well. I'm sure your brother—BB, is it?—wouldn't want you to feel bad for him."

"I don't know what BB is feeling. He can't come home and tell me. I can't even see him."

The teacher stepped back in surprise. "Why is that?"

Ben slashed more black across a new page. "Because of the foster babies. If BB comes around, the agency may think he's a bad influence and take the babies away from Dad and Wendy." Ben scowled all the way to his feet. "I'd rather have BB than the babies."

Mrs. Wellford's voice came back gentle. "You said you love the babies."

Ben's voice broke. "I do. I don't want to choose between them, but if I have to, I'd rather have BB." Water stung his eyes. *It's not fair, God. It's not. I don't want to choose. I want them all—the babies and my brother. Please don't make it one or the other. You can change this. You can solve this. Make it all go away. Have the scumbag who lied about BB tell the truth. That will fix it. Won't it? I know You can make whoever it is do it. You can.*

Dad says You can do anything. But You don't always do it the way we want it. Please. I want my brother back. And I want Dad and Wendy to have the babies, too. Will You do that for me? For us? Please? I know I have to ask for Your will. Please.

Mrs. Wellford put her hand on Ben's back and rubbed it. He lowered his head and wiped his eyes on his sleeve. He looked up and swallowed hard. Then he said, "I'm better now."

"I know you are, Ben. You're a strong young man. Your family will come through this. You'll see." She stopped, removed her hand, and added, "You can always talk to me, Ben. Even during school if you need to. Just tell your teacher you need to see me. I'll talk to you."

Ben nodded. He took out another piece of paper and started another drawing. In pencil.

After class, he ran into Tricia. She looked sad. Her eyes were red. Ben cocked his head to the side, "What's wrong?"

Tricia lowered her eyes. "My mom says I can't go to your house anymore."

Ben kicked the tarmac. "Because of the lies about my brother?"

She nodded. "Yeah." Tricia hugged her books with both arms.

Ben threw his books on the ground. "BB didn't do anything wrong. People are lying about him. Doesn't your mom care about what's true?"

Tricia stepped away. "I'm sorry, Ben. I like you. I liked going with you to church. But my mom—"

Ben shouted, "Your mom is like everyone else! They want to believe the lies and don't care about the real truth."

Craig came up behind them. "Truth? Your brother murdered a dealer and took over his territory?"

Ben shoved Craig into the wall. He yelled, "My brother didn't kill anyone! He's not a drug dealer! He loves Jesus. He'd never do that."

Craig took a swing at Ben. Ben ducked. Craig crowded him, trying to force Ben up against the wall. Ben danced away, keeping his distance from the building. Craig would pound him if he had the chance. Ben had to stay out of his reach.

Craig threw another punch. Ben ducked. Craig's fist made contact with the wall. The force of the blow dropped Craig to his knees in pain. He howled and grabbed his hand to cradle it.

The noise brought a yard monitor. The man got between Ben and the sobbing Craig. "What's going on?"

Tricia backed Ben. "Craig swung at Ben. Ben ducked and Craig hit the wall."

Craig shouted, "I'm gonna kill you, you punk! Just like your brother killed—"

The teacher, Mr. Pulliam, caught Craig by the arm. "That's enough. I think I know what's happening." He pulled Craig's hand away from him to look at it. The fist bled from three fingers.

Craig continued to spew threats as Mr. Pullium led him away. The man looked at Ben and said, "Report to the office. Tell them what happened. I'll be along as soon as I get Craig to the nurse."

Ben gathered his books from the ground. Tricia lifted her head. "I'll go with you. I can back up your story."

Ben's anger almost snapped. But the Lord sat on his tongue. Ben nodded. "Thanks. Thanks for saying what you did to Mr. Pulliam."

"It's the truth. I care about what is true." She fell in step with Ben as he walked toward the office.

Ben kept his head down but looked at Tricia. "Don't you care what people will think?"

She tossed her curls. "No, I don't. Let them think what they want. Your brother didn't do anything, and neither did you." Her eyes hardened. "My dad says to stick up for what I believe. Well, I'm sticking up for it. So there."

Ben smiled but only a little. He muttered, "Thanks, Tricia. I appreciate you."

She nodded her head sharply. "You better." And she smiled.

* * *

FRIDAY

BB showed up at the Mission at six. He wanted to be there before all the other volunteers came in. Made it less awkward. The others would have to decide whether to greet him or not. But he would be there and working.

Dee opened the door to let him in. "You're bright and early."

"Early, anyhow. I'll be bright after a good cup of coffee." He went to the back of the kitchen and pulled up the coffee pot. The closing crew had cleaned it and left it ready for the morning bunch. All he needed was to plug it in and turn it on. BB added another scoop of grounds to the premeasured mound. Evening crew never made it strong enough. BB wanted to match his dad's taste. Once brewed, it could always be watered down. But you can't make it stronger. Dad taught him that. And BB had learned well.

He pulled out the eggs, bacon, potatoes, onions, salt, and pepper. He set about to chop the potatoes into chunks suitable for frying with the onions and the bacon.

Halfway through dicing five pounds of spuds, his dad walked in. Wendy followed close behind him. No babies. BB's eyes widened. He motioned to Wendy. "Where are the fosters?"

Wendy's voice was sharp. "Social media. Someone

posted that we were foster parents. Someone else made the connection with you. Then the harassment started about our reasons for fostering…and our fitness to be parents." Her voice caught. "It got ugly. Then it got uglier. I had maybe fifty comments on my personal page before I shut it down. All of them negative." Her eyes burned. "They even accused us of getting one of the babies hooked on crack." Her fire faded. "So, yeah, no babies."

Dad slipped in around the knife and hugged BB. He explained, "The agency decided to withdraw the children while they investigated the rumors. They want to wait for the police investigation to be finished."

BB processed the information. His anger burned. He swallowed it. He dropped his head but said none of the things he wanted to.

Dad asked, "How'd it go last night at the dorm?"

BB shook his head. "Room was asleep when I got home. Still sleeping when I left. I haven't talked with anyone yet." He paused, then added, "I did text Julie. She said she'd come here this morning rather than talk Wednesday night."

Dad's eyebrows went up, but he said only, "Oh. That will be interesting."

BB nodded. "Yeah, it will be. At least I'll be surrounded by supporters. You can keep me straight."

Dad smiled. "I trust you to keep yourself in control."

BB didn't. He hesitated. "How's Ben?"

Wendy looked at Dad, then said, "He had a little trouble at school. But the boy who has been taunting him all year is gone. Maybe it will be better for Ben."

"Gone? How? Why?" Had something good really come from this? At least for Ben?

"Expelled. He took a swing at Ben. The school has zero tolerance for violence. And Craig's been in trouble before. Multiple times. Ben wasn't his only target."

"Did he hit Ben?" BB's gut tightened.

Wendy smiled and then swallowed it. "Craig missed

Ben and hit the wall. Three broken knuckles and two bones in his hand cracked. He won't be hitting anyone else for some time. And he'll be homeschooled the remainder of the year."

BB let out a sigh. Okay, something positive had come out of this. Ben had been relieved of a bully. Wendy wasn't done. "It seems Tricia stood up for Ben. They've become very good friends. She even stood up to her mother about Ben and you. I think Ben's got a good one."

BB groused, "Lucky him." He looked up and added, "No, I'm glad for him. It's good he's got someone in his corner at school."

Dad shrugged. "Even if she is a girl."

Wendy threatened, "Now, let's not go there." The levity between his parents—yes, he'd call them that—helped take the edge off. At least until someone mentioned the rumor or said something to remind him.

Dad began chopping the onions. Wendy joined BB in slicing the potatoes into chunks. Dad said, "I'm sure this will be resolved when the police finish their investigation. The need for foster parents is great. The rumor may not go away, but the proof will be enough to reinstate us. We'll take it a day at a time."

Dad's confidence irked BB. He scowled. "Doesn't this rattle you at all?"

Dad laid the knife on the counter. "Of course it does. Someone is throwing accusations about my son. My family could be torn apart." BB heard the anguish in his dad's voice. It wasn't how he wanted his dad to feel…but it was, in a sense, reassuring. Dad was human. He understood.

BB gave his attention to the food prep and began placing everything in a metal pan for cooking. The bacon needed to be fried first, so it went to the griddle. They could cook it in the oven, but the grill cooked faster. He cut the strips into chunks to mix into the potatoes.

At eight, the remainder of the breakfast crew filed in.

BB held his breath, but no one said anything or acted as if things were out of the ordinary. Either they hadn't heard, or they were ignoring it. For now? For better or worse.

The patrons began to file in just after eight-thirty. Intent on getting to the food before it ran out. Not that it ever did. The Mission's benefactors made sure the food lasted through each meal and into the next. No shortages. No one turned away. No judgment.

But no smoking, no matter what they brought. No fighting. No making a scene. BB watched a woman come in with her three preschool-age children. The littles tried to sit and eat. But at that age, everything and everyone became a distraction. Cheerios were tossed across the table. Mom tried to redirect. A child began to cry. Milk spilled.

An older woman with blue-tinted hair and an attitude of entitlement complained for all to hear, "She should keep control of those brats. My children never acted out like that."

BB saw Wendy move from the kitchen to the dining area. She sat next to the harried mother and smiled. "Welcome. I haven't seen you here before. How can I help?"

Gratitude washed over the woman's face. She handed the youngest, possibly a two-year-old, to Wendy. "Thank you so much. It's the first proper meal they've had since yesterday morning."

Wendy took the child. "Then let's make sure they get it in them, not just on them." She began to feed the child finger foods.

Another female volunteer, Mandy, came up beside the woman and asked, "Would you like some coffee?"

The mother sighed. "I would love some. I can't balance the kids' trays and hot coffee at the same time."

The volunteer smiled. "Been there, couldn't do it, either. Let me get you a cup. With coffee in it. Black? Creamer?"

"Just black. Thank you so much."

Mandy walked to the coffee pot past the complaining

woman. She hummed, "Jesus loves the little children," as she passed.

Daggers would have been thrown if there had been any. But the blunt silverware the Mission used was suitable for eating, not something anyone could readily use as a weapon. Ms. Entitled could only stew and stare in Mandy's direction.

Mandy came back with a cup and a carafe of coffee. She poured some for the mother, then motioned toward the complaining woman's cup as well. She smiled. "I see your cup is empty. Let me fill it."

From the back, Pastor Dee walked up. He nodded to Mandy, nodded to Wendy, then caught Ms. Entitled's eyes and said, "And that is how we become the hands and feet of our Lord."

The older woman huffed but accepted the coffee. And kept her opinions to herself. BB kept his smirk to himself. *Well played, Dee. Well played.*

He retrieved several trays and plates left behind on tables. As he returned from the kitchen, he saw Julie talking with Wendy. Hmm. Their discussion could go so many ways. He decided to disappear into the kitchen and wait for Julie to approach him. If she wanted.

It took a few minutes, but Julie came into the area looking for him. Her face reflected concern and maybe sadness. BB smiled at her. "Hey, beautiful."

She looked up and came in for a hug. She buried her head in his chest and held him for several moments. When she looked up, she whispered, "I'm so sorry. I am."

BB studied her a moment, then guessed, "Wendy told you they lost the babies because of me, didn't she?"

Julie nodded. Her voice caught. "I had no idea a rumor could hurt you like that." Her eyes appeared hollow.

BB gave her a straight-lipped smile. "Not just me. My parents, my brother, the triplets. All the foster children who never get the chance for a real home. It trickles down. My folks could have offered those kids a permanent place to live, grow, and get real schooling."

He leaned against the counter. "I'm not saying they're the only couple who can offer that. But they'll never have the chance now."

Julie's eyes filled with moisture. "This will blow over. I'm sure it will."

BB shook his head. "No, this rumor will go with me forever. It's like being accused of child abuse. Even if the facts are shown to be false, people will think, 'There must have been some truth to it…where there's smoke, there's fire.' It will always be there."

Tears trickled down her cheek. "I'm so sorry, BB. I don't know what to say."

BB touched her cheek. Servers bustled around them. Trays of lettuce and tomatoes passed by on their way to be made into sandwiches. Calls of, "Whose got the mayo?" "Where's the mustard?" were tossed across the room. BB and Julie were in a swirl of action yet somehow separate from it.

BB asked, "Can you tell me where the rumor started? Who started it? Or who did you hear it from?"

Julie stared at the floor. "I just heard it. You know…people talking. Someone at the cafeteria said they heard about the dead body. Someone else said he was a drug dealer. The talk went to you flashing cash in front of Leeland and Samuel. A guy said everyone knew you were the one who killed him…no one has that kind of cash. Especially not to pay off someone else's debt. You had to be in on it. That you're dangerous."

She looked into BB's eyes. "I swear it, BB. I heard it as I walked by. That's all. I don't know how they knew about Leeland and the money. Maybe he said something to someone about it. He had to be pretty happy about being free from Vic."

BB shook his head. "I'm sure he must have been. But I'm sure he didn't go out telling people he got bought out from under service to another student. He probably didn't want anyone to know he'd been in debt to begin with." BB didn't mention the scholarship. And how Leeland still asked what he had to do to make up for the help. No matter how many times BB told him it was a gift, Leeland still looked for the "gotcha."

Julie shrugged, her shoulders tight. "I don't know, then. If it wasn't Leeland, maybe Samuel said something? Maybe he became jealous you didn't give him money, too."

BB knew better. "Samuel earns his own way. He's very definite about not being in debt to anyone for anything. Not even breakfast. He told me if he can't earn it, he doesn't deserve it."

Julie squared her shoulders. "You think Vic would do this? He's a lowlife, but I can't see him trying to destroy someone. Especially his roommate. He has to live with you. He wouldn't do anything like this."

BB rubbed his hand over his jaw. "We have different opinions of what Vic will and won't do. He doesn't want me in the dorm. I cramp his style. He'd be more than happy if I were gone."

Julie stared at BB. "What are you going to do?"

BB held out his hands wide. "What can I do? The genie is out of the bottle. No matter what I say, or even if Vic were to deny it, the mere accusation is enough for most people. Having Vic recant won't make a difference. I've got to live with it. And trust myself to the One Who judges righteously."

Julie avoided BB's eyes. "You mean Jesus. He's not exactly helping you, is he?"

"He's with me. He knows what I'm going through. He's been through it and worse. I trust Him to have a plan."

Julie looked up in shock. "That's it? You go through this, and you still trust him? It's not fair. It's not right. The Lord could have stopped it if he wanted to, but he didn't. What does that say about him?" Derision filled her tone.

BB smiled slightly. "It says He knows something I don't. Even in this darkness, I still trust Him. He knows, I don't."

Julie shook her head from side to side. "I don't believe you. Your parents are obviously hurting. How is this affecting your brother? It has to be embarrassing to him. Being a kid of what, thirteen? Fourteen? I'd be crushed if my brother got accused of dealing drugs. Even if it wasn't true, the accusation alone—"

"Would be damaging. I know. He's having a tough time at school. But he's got friends who are backing him. People who know him and me are sticking up for him."

BB pointed around the kitchen. "No one here has said a word to me. They all know me. They have my back. Pastor Dee and I talked Wednesday night. I'll continue to serve no matter what. And I'll stand before the congregation on Sunday and declare the truth that the rumor is out there, but it's a lie. And anyone can ask me about it."

Julie's eyes widened. "You're going to stand in front of the church and tell everyone?"

"Yeah, I'm going before them. I know how it will go. Our church is a family. This is family business. We'll handle it in love."

She shook her head. "So, none of this will affect you? Jesus makes it all go away." Her eyes narrowed and disbelief colored her face.

BB kept frustration from painting his tone shades he didn't want to express. "It doesn't all 'go away.' The consequences are still out there. It's already hurt my folks. It hurt my brother. It hurt me. But it won't destroy any of us. We'll learn from it. We'll grow from it. And we'll come away stronger. You know the swords, 'even if'? Even if the Lord didn't rescue the three men in the fire, they wouldn't deny the Lord. Well, even if this doesn't go away, I'm still going to follow Jesus."

Julie hugged him. "You're something else, BB Andres.

I don't know what yet, but you are." She let him go and then looked around. "I think you've got things pretty well in hand here. I'm going to leave and get some studying done."

BB kissed the top of her head. "Thanks for coming by. I appreciate it. I'll talk to you later." He stopped and added, "If you don't think hanging with a drug dealer will affect your reputation." The jest fell flat even as he said it.

She smirked. "I'll have to think about it." She kissed her fingers, swiped them across BB's lips, and walked out.

BB sagged against the counter. He became aware of the ebb and flow of life around him again. Lunch prep continued in full swing. He needed to get busy. Life moved on.

At two, he called it quits. He had a paper to turn in, and an appointment with his advisor to review it. As much as he hated leaving, classes were still a reality. Would his advisor have heard the rumors? Would he want to work with BB? Time and interaction would tell. But first, BB had to return to the dorm. Facing Vic would be the next problem.

Twenty minutes across town and a five-minute walk from the parking lot wasn't enough time to figure out what to say. He bathed every minute in prayer to take away his anger, keep from pummeling Vic, and be a worthy representative of Christ. BB stopped at the door and took in a deep breath. He opened the door and pushed through it.

Vic sat at his desk watching videos. He looked up as BB came in and shut down the laptop. "Hey, loser."

"Vic." BB looked around. "Where's Samuel?" Did the lineman have anything to do with spreading the rumors?

"In class. Might surprise you we do sometimes go."

BB grinned in spite of himself. "Not often."

"Granted." Vic turned away from BB and went back to his videos.

BB eyed Vic from the back. What was going on? No comments? No insults. More than normal. No innuendo about the drug dealer? Had the Lord worked a miracle?

BB went to his desk and picked up his books. He made

sure he had all his assignments and papers. Then he turned to go. "I'll see you tonight, I guess."

Vic nodded. "Call before you come. I might have company."

"I'll do that." BB walked out, closing the door behind him. He leaned against the wall and gathered himself. *Lord? Did You do a work in his life? Why isn't he crowing about bringing me down? Why isn't he rubbing it in about the rumors? Something's not right here. But if this is You, thank You.*

BB headed to the science building.

***

SUNDAY

Sunday at the Mission. BB, Ben, Wendy, and Dad sat in the front row of chairs. Word had spread BB would be attending. The seats were full. Some wanted a look at a murderer. Some wanted to see a scene as the police dragged him out. Some came in support of BB's innocence. A few came because it was Sunday, and that's what you do.

Pastor DeWayne delivered the message from the book of James. "The tongue is a fire…" When he finished, he called BB to the front.

Gasps sounded from the congregation as BB walked up to the podium. He took the microphone from Pastor Dee and looked out over the assembly. He saw faces he knew. Faces he didn't. Faces he thought he recognized but couldn't be sure. And one face totally out of place. BB's eyes widened. He looked at the floor. He had a job to do. No distractions.

BB inhaled. He waited, exhaled, and then said, "I did not kill Jamis Fenton. I didn't know the name of the man who died before now. I don't know anything about how he died or why he died. I do not deal narcotics or drugs of any kind. If you have heard those rumors, they're false. And if you have heard them, please come to me and tell me who you heard them from. I want to end these whispers once and for all. My family is hurting because of the lies that are being circulated. If you don't want to talk to me, talk to Pastor Dee. Tell him where you heard it. But this must stop. As your brother in the Lord, I'm begging you. Please." He laid the mic down, stepped from the podium, and sat back in his seat.

Dee picked up the mic. "You heard our brother. Tell the truth. Let's end this. Today." He gazed over the assembly. "Let's pray. Lord, You alone know what You intend with these rumors. We battle not against flesh and blood, but against spiritual wickedness in dark places. Nothing pleases our enemy more than lies in the dark. Only Your light can dispel the darkness. Shine Your light for all to see. Illuminate the truth. Redeem even this for Your glory. We ask it all in Your Name, amen." He looked at the congregation. "You're dismissed."

BB stood quickly to watch the back door. A familiar figure—in a very unfamiliar place—walked out. BB closed his eyes. Was this Vic's revenge for Leeland's freedom? Had the man orchestrated this, and now, having seen BB's comeuppance, would he be satisfied?

A woman tapped BB on the shoulder. He looked at her. It took him a moment until he smiled. "Tamara! I prayed you'd find your way here." He lost the smile. "I didn't expect you to have to see this, though." Her clothes were more modest than the night he'd met her on the street in front of the restaurant.

She shrugged. "A bad day at church is still a good day, right?"

He nodded. "Let me introduce you to my family."

Her eyes crinkled. "You're going to introduce a street walker to your family? Boy, you need to work on your people skills."

He grabbed Dad's arm. "Dad. Wendy. This is Tamara, and I never got her last name. I met her outside the restaurant a couple of weeks ago. When you came to pick me up, Wendy."

Dad held out his hand. "Nice to meet you. I'm Mick

Andres." Wendy smiled and said, "Welcome." Ben stared at his feet.

Tamara shook Dad's hand. She looked at Dad, then at BB, then at Ben, then at Dad again. The age difference. But she said only, "Interesting service this morning." She looked pointedly at BB. "Is there a place we can get a few private words?" She stopped, then added, "With your folks, of course."

BB jerked his head to the side. "Sure. We can go in the prayer room." He smiled a straight-lipped smile. "It's usually empty."

The party of five moved to the room off the main assembly hall. BB shut the door after everyone had come in. He asked, "Is this a sit-down kind of meeting?"

Tamara shrugged. "I won't be long." She looked at BB, then at Dad. "You have an outstanding son here. And I can say without fear of contradiction, he had nothing to do with the death of Jamis Fenton." She paused, then added, "And no, you can't ask how I know. I do." Her lips pursed. "That's all I can say."

BB felt his knees shake. They wanted to buckle, but he held himself upright. "Thank you." He shook her hand. "Thank you." He hugged her. Then stepped back in embarrassment.

Tamara laughed and shrugged. "I don't know who started the rumor. The investigation is ongoing. There's still a note being examined. When the police report is released, you'll be exonerated." She looked at Dad and Wendy. "But you didn't hear it from me."

Wendy breathed out, "Praise the Lord. Thank you."

Ben raised his eyes long enough to say, "I knew he was innocent. The police didn't have to tell me."

Tamara looked at BB. "You impressed me the other night. I knew I had to say something when I heard you being accused. I came down here looking for you. I didn't expect to find you on trial." The woman shook her head. Her eyes glimmered in anger.

Wendy's tone sounded dry. "He'd get a fairer shake in a real trial. Public opinion is much harder to buck."

Dad laid a hand on Wendy's arm. He squeezed it, then told Tamara, "I appreciate you standing up for BB's defense. We won't share what you've told us." He raised his eyebrows. "You're taking a chance coming here like this. I appreciate it more than you know."

"What? A streetwalker can't come to a mission church?" Tamara's eyes twinkled. She glanced around the empty room. A portable blackboard had names written on it, with notes beside them: mother ill. Sister having baby. Family finances. The prayer list went on.

Dad laughed. "Of course, she can. But they don't normally pack a gun and a badge."

Her eyes narrowed. She stared hard at Dad, then asked softly, "Let's not talk about that part."

Dad nodded. "Not a word."

Tamara laughed. "Am I so obvious?"

"Not at all. Takes a trained eye." He smiled. "Trained by the best."

Tamara's eyebrows lifted. "We'll have to discuss that sometime."

Dad grinned. "Any time."

Ben looked up for a moment, then stared at the floor again. "We will get my baby sisters and brothers back."

His tone lacked conviction. Or color. Something bothered him. BB didn't know what, but something was off. He'd have to ask when they went home. And he would go home today.

Tamara said, "I'd better go." She chuckled. "Don't want to start any more rumors."

Dad reached in and hugged Tamara. "Thank you again for coming to BB's aide. Be careful out there. And come by any time."

BB opened the door and whispered, "Thank you," as

Tamara exited the room.

The family gave the woman a few moments head start, then returned to the assembly room. People were still filing out or filing into the dining area for a noon meal. BB and crew headed to the kitchen to continue food prep. One group of volunteers had already started laying out the supplies for ham and scalloped potatoes. The morning worshippers would finish while the early crew went to service. Everyone shared the duties.

BB kept an eye on Ben. His brother seemed unnaturally quiet. Morose, even. Unusual for Ben. BB shifted stations to be close to him. He studied him, then asked, "You okay, bro?"

Ben hung his head lower. "I'm fine."

Which was code in the family for, "I'm not, but I don't want to talk about it right now."

BB sucked in his bottom lip. How to get his brother to talk to him? Being down like this was not part of Ben's makeup. Had something more happened at school? Had Tricia's mother forbidden them to talk to one another? Not that she could enforce it, but still, with the threat there, Ben would want to obey the edict out of respect. Even if it meant not talking to Tricia. Could she be causing Ben grief?

BB would have to wait and try to ask again later. And hope his dad had better luck getting Ben to talk. If he could. For now, he had a ham to carve. Plates to serve. Potatoes to dish up. Mouths to feed. Sunday. *Thank You, Lord, we get to serve. Use us and this food for Your purposes.* BB went back to work.

* * *

BB checked in at the dorm later in the evening. With a class early in the morning, it would be easier to sleep at the dorm than at home.

Vic lay on Samuel's upper bunk. He stared at the ceiling above him, tossing a football into the air and catching it. BB dropped his books on his desk, shoved Leeland's dirty socks off the bed opposite Vic, and sat. He studied his roommate.

Vic looked over at him, then returned to staring at the ceiling. BB tried breaking the mood. "Hey. Saw you at church this morning."

Vic nodded. "Wanted to see how the other half lived." He looked over at BB. "Nice speech. Too bad you had to make it."

BB tried to match Vic's energy. "Yeah, well, sometimes a rumor gets out of hand."

Vic stared at the wall. "Sometimes they get started on purpose." He looked up at BB. "It wasn't me." He lay back and tossed the ball in the air. "I know you didn't kill the guy."

BB eased his legs out straight. The strong odor of stinky socks wafted to perfume the air, even with the offending garments on the floor. "Thanks. How do you know?"

Vic shot up to a sitting position. His face contorted into anger and shame. "I know Jamis Fenton. He killed himself. His note said so." He stared into BB's face. "Because of me." He threw the ball against the far wall with enough force to crack the mirror.

BB's eyes widened. He looked at the mirror, then back to Vic. "What?"

Vic stared at the floor. He looked exactly like Ben, refusing to look at BB. "He owed me money." Vic laughed, but harshly. "Who doesn't?" He stopped. "You don't. I know." He went back to looking at the floor. BB shifted on the bed. Quietly so as not to disturb Vic's story.

"He wasn't paying me back. Couldn't pay what he didn't have. Yeah, well, I've heard that story before. And I knew better. So I threatened him. Told him I'd out him to his parents if he didn't pay up."

BB's eyes widened. He said nothing. Vic's voice broke. "How would I know he'd take his life? He wrote a letter. Said his folks would kill him, so he may as well do the job first. And it would be my fault. I'd have to live with it. The police have the letter. My name is in it. They came and asked me questions. And told me what Jamis said." Vic buried his head in his hands. "Thing is, his parents already knew. They didn't care. They were waiting for him to tell them himself. So they could put it behind them."

The distraught man looked up, and though tears burned in his eyes, his voice sounded fierce. "Don't tell me it wasn't my fault. Tell me how to live with it."

BB leaned forward and put his elbows on his knees. "You don't. You give it up."

"That's so easy, right? You do something wrong, you ask forgiveness, and you go on like nothing happened. Get out of jail free card. Well, I don't believe that." Harsh. The man's voice came out harsh. With a note of anguish.

BB kept his voice even. "I don't believe that, either. Someone has to pay for it." He asked, "You want to pay for it yourself? Let his folks kill you in exchange for their son's life?"

Vic stared at BB, his voice incredulous. "What?"

BB nodded. "Jamis died. Someone has to pay for it. Should it be you? But if his folks take your life, who should take theirs?"

Vic shook his head. "You're talking crazy."

"No, I'm telling you what is. The penalty for causing someone to die is death. Whether you intended it or not doesn't matter. In God's economy, someone has to pay for it." Vic's eyes widened, then hardened, then stared at the floor. BB softened his voice. "Which was why Jesus came. He took the penalty for all the wrongs. And it cost Him everything. His status. His position. His life. Tortured. Spit on. Mocked. The King of Heaven treated like a common criminal." BB's voice caught. "Because of what you and I did. And do. It's not a 'get out of jail free' card. It's an 'it cost Him everything, so we owe Him everything' card."

Vic slid off the bed to his bunk to sit opposite BB. "Yeah? What's he get out of the deal?"

"Your soul. Safe for all eternity."

"You mean I gotta live like you? No thanks." Disgust. Maybe with a shade of longing.

"How you live is between you and God. You give Him your life, and He directs you. My path isn't yours. You're you, completely unique. That's how God created you. And your path will be unique as well."

Vic studied a knuckle on his hand. "Yeah? How's that work?"

"When you give Him your life, He gives you His Spirit. The Companion and Counselor. He will be the One Who guides you into what He wants you to do."

"And what if I don't want to do it?"

"That's between you and Him. Ever hear of Jonah?"

"The dude with the big fish? Yeah, I know that story. Learned it in kindergarten."

"Then you know God told Jonah to go to a certain city. Jonah said no and went the other way. God had him swallowed by a big fish to give him time to change his mind. Jonah thought about it and decided he should maybe go."

Vic snorted. "Yeah, well, who wouldn't?"

"The point is, God gave Jonah a second chance. Once Jonah got free from the fish, God told him again to go. Jonah went but with a bad attitude. He grumbled and complained and was full of hate. God got the message across to the city, and the people were spared. But Jonah continued to be miserable and obstinate. He had free will. Just like you do and will. You can always say no to God. Even after you give Him your life. You may not like the consequences., but it's always your choice."

"And what do I get out of it? If I 'give him my soul,' I mean?"

"Life. Light. Joy." BB's voice caught. "All of Heaven. A Companion Who will never leave you, ever. Never being alone again. Peace."

Vic fell silent. After a moment, he asked, "What made

you decide?"

BB chuckled. "I got 'adopted' by a bunch who lived and breathed Jesus. I saw how they faced life. They had a peace despite everything going wrong around them. They loved, they hurt, they fought, they argued…but they had this joy. I wanted it. Then I found out there wasn't an 'it,' there was a Person. Jesus. I gave Him my life, and I've never regretted it. Or Him."

Vic studied BB. "What do you get out of it? If I decide, I mean? You get to brag to your friends how you 'saved' me?"

BB remained patient. And honest. "I get nothing out of it, Vic. I didn't do anything. God gets all the credit. Someone plants a seed. Someone waters the seed. But if God doesn't make it grow, nothing happens. God does all the work. Sometimes, I get to see it when God brings someone to Himself. Most times, not. The point isn't to see how many we draw. The point is to see people accept Christ."

Vic shifted on the bunk. He stared at the floor. "Do I have to say something special? Specific words?"

"'God help me' works. It's what's in your heart, Vic. You can say all the 'right words' and still not be saved. It's what's in here." BB pointed to the center of his chest and patted it. "Deep here. And God will honor it."

Vic looked to the side, looked to the other side, looked at the floor, and then looked at BB. "You don't get to tell everyone. Or anyone. Right?"

BB held up his hand. "I won't tell a soul without your permission. But you will. When you accept Him, you'll want to tell everyone who will listen. It's just that way."

Vic stood. "I'll think about it." He headed to his desk and then pointed at the mirror. "You should probably clean the mess up."

BB suppressed the grin. "I'll get right on it." Vic grabbed his football and disappeared out the door. BB shook his head. "He's all Yours, Lord. Do Your work. You know his heart. Only You can reach him."

BB stood and walked to his desk. He should be studying The Western Tradition of Justice and the Law. But praying seemed more important. He sat down, bowed his head, and began. "Father, I praise You for all You've done. And all You continue to do. Be with Vic. Be with the Fenton family. And be with whoever started the rumors. Change their heart, Lord. Reach them. And if it serves you, clear my name."

He paused, then began again. "Bless Dad, Wendy, Ben, Tav, Jen, and all the Knights. Be with Popdad…"

And on and on and on.

* * *

MONDAY

You screwed up.
I did what you said. He's not budging.
Think of something. Be creative. I want him taken down.

Ben stepped off the bus and saw Tricia waiting for him. Wonderful. Just who he didn't want to see first thing Monday morning. Not when he had so much on his mind. His brother standing up for Jesus on Sunday had been bad enough.

She rushed up to meet him. "Did you hear about Craig? He got expelled. They warned him, and then they did it." She almost danced. "No more bullies."

Ben lowered his head and muttered, "Yeah."

Tricia walked beside him. "What's wrong? Aren't you happy he's gone?"

Ben gave her a side-eye, then looked at the ground. "Yeah."

Tricia stopped walking. "Ben Andres, what is wrong with you?" She put her free hand on her hip. The other held her books.

Ben scowled. "I'll tell you at lunch." He hurried ahead to get to class. Not that he would be late, but he wanted to get away from Tricia. Her presence reminded him too much of his…transgression, Dad would call it. And Ben didn't want to think about it. He wanted to forget it ever happened.

He couldn't pay attention in history class. He kept thinking of how Dad and Wendy would be disappointed in him. He'd let them down. BB stood up for what he knew was right. Ben had lied…

Okay, he hadn't lied. But he hadn't told the truth. Not the whole truth. When Tricia said Craig tried to hit Ben, she told the truth. But she didn't say Ben pushed Craig. She didn't tell the whole truth.

And Ben had gone along with it. He didn't mean to at the time. Craig's hand had been broken and bleeding, and Mr. Pullium pulled him away to the nurse's office. Ben didn't think about what Tricia said at the time.

But he thought about it Thursday night. And Friday. And Saturday and Sunday. He couldn't get past the feeling he'd done a terrible thing and needed to confess. But he was afraid. Afraid they would expel him, too. He started the fight. It had to be his fault. He should…he should…

"Mr. Andres, are you going to sit here through next period? Or are you going to math?"

Ben looked up at Ms. Stark. The bell had rung, and everyone had left. He rose to his feet. "I'm going."

"Thank you." She studied him a moment, her head cocked to the side. "Is there something bothering you?"

"No." Ben lowered his head, then corrected himself. "No, ma'am."

She smiled a little. "Thank you, Ben. I have to say, you're one of the politest students I have."

Ben gathered his books. "Thank you, Ms. Stark." He hurried out of the room before he'd have to say thank you another time. Besides, he didn't deserve to be told how good he was. He wasn't. He was terrible.

Art proved the worst. Nothing he drew looked like anything. They were supposed to draw a family composition. Ben couldn't draw himself. Not sitting with his parents. They wouldn't want anything to do with him when they found out what a liar he had been. Though he hadn't lied. Tricia had. Would it make a difference to them?

They were so proud of BB. They would be so disappointed in him. It didn't matter that Dad said he loved Ben no matter what. "Unconditionally," he said. Dad always showed how much he loved Ben, even when Ben had done something wrong. But this might be different. He knew it would be. He knew it. The whisper in his ear told him so. There could be no family picture. Only Dad, Wendy, and BB. BB deserved to be there. Ben didn't.

Lunch came after art. Lunch meant facing Tricia. He tried to hide from her, but she found him. She glared at him. "You owe me an explanation. What's wrong?"

Could he lie to Tricia? He'd already lied to Mr. Pullium.

But he hadn't lied. He didn't speak up when Tricia said Craig tried to hit Ben. Which meant she didn't lie, either. She didn't tell the whole truth, and Ben didn't correct her. Had it been the same as lying?

He kicked at the dirt. "You didn't tell Mr. Pullium I shoved Craig. It might mean what happened could be partly my fault."

Tricia scoffed. "Is that all? You didn't swing at him. He swung at you. Pushing someone isn't the same thing at all. And Craig had it coming. He said all those bad things about your brother. You weren't to blame."

Ben stared at her. "Then it won't matter if I go to Mr. Pullium and tell him I started the fight." Relief flooded him.

Tricia's eyes widened. "You can't do that! You can't. What if they expel you, too? I wouldn't have anyone to talk to. I'd lose my only friend."

Ben stared her up and down. "I'm not your only friend. You have lots of people who like you." She usually had lots of people around her. She must have somehow ditched them to talk to him. But why? She couldn't tell people she spent time with Ben. That would be terrible. For her, anyhow. No one would like her if they knew.

Tricia's voice snapped, "They like me because I'm popular. They think that will make them popular, too. You like me because I'm me." She pleaded, "You can't tell them you started the fight. You can't. Promise me you won't say anything. Please? Please?"

Ben locked his eyes on the ground. "I have to tell someone. I feel lousy inside about it."

"Tell me. And I'm the only one who needs to know. It'll be our secret."

Ben's head jerked up. "No! No secrets. Dad says keeping secrets is wrong." He stopped. "Some kinds of secrets are okay, like what we got each other for a present or something. But we don't keep secrets at our house. I can't promise that."

Tricia tossed her head. "I keep secrets from my dad and mom all the time. They don't need to know everything I do." She paused. "Like Mom doesn't know I'm talking to you. She said I shouldn't. But I don't care what she says. You're my friend, and I'm going to talk to you."

"Your mom said we can't talk?"

"Yeah. But she can't stop me."

Ben's stomach lurched. First, he didn't tell about starting the fight. Now, he had broken another parent's rules about their kid. Could he get any worse?

Tricia continued to yammer in his ear. "You can't tell anyone, Ben. You can't. I won't lose a friend. Not a friend like you. Promise me you won't tell your folks. I won't tell my mom we're talking, and you won't tell your parents about starting the fight, right? We'll both keep it quiet. We won't lie. We just won't tell them."

Ben shook his head. "You don't understand. I'm a Knight of the Octagon. We don't lie."

Tricia laughed. "I don't care about some silly game you play. Knight of the what? Everyone lies about something. It's not a big deal."

Ben shook his head. "Someone lied about my brother.

That was a big deal."

"But that's different. They meant it to be mean. Malicious. I'm not saying we lie to anyone. We just don't tell them the whole truth."

Ben knew she was wrong. Not telling the whole truth would be as bad as lying. He knew it. He'd been taught it. Jesus wouldn't like it.

Tricia didn't understand. Ben couldn't make her understand, either. He would promise not to tell his parents. But he would tell BB. BB would help him know what he should do.

He rubbed his hand across his face. "I won't tell my folks about this."

"Promise me you won't tell anyone."

Ben drew in a deep breath and exhaled slowly. He needed to take a stand. "I can't promise you. I promise I won't tell my parents. That's all."

Tricia sagged. "I guess that's as good as I'm going to get. We better get to class. And cheer up. Nothing is going to happen to you. Everything will be fine. You'll see." She reached in and gave him a quick peck on the cheek, then raced off to class.

Ben's eyes widened. He touched his face where she'd brushed it with her lips. A girl kissed him. A girl kissed him. He floated down the hall to his next class.

* * *

BB walked out of his last class. Spring warmed the air. Student voices filled it. BB breathed deeply and headed to the dorm. He reached into his pocket for his phone.

Something struck him in the neck from behind. Stunned, BB went to his knees. A man's voice shouted, "That's for Jamis, you coward!"

BB curled back and grabbed his assailant's legs at the knee, pulling him forward and knocking him to the ground. He rolled to his right and came to his feet. All of Quinn Magary's training flooded his mind. *No fear. An attacker from the back is more frightened than you are. Be calm. Deescalate if you can.*

BB could see the young man's face filled with hate. And tears. BB kept his voice even. "I did not kill Jamis Fenton. He wasn't a drug dealer, and I didn't kill him."

The man stood only slightly taller than BB. BB could take him if it came to it. He hoped it wouldn't. The man's hands shook in time to his voice. "You would say that. No one ever accused Jamis of being a drug dealer until you killed him."

The man swung again. BB ducked under the swing and came up behind the man. He caught the hapless attacker under the shoulders and behind the neck. BB forced the man's head down just far enough to hold him, mindful of staying out of kicking range. "Listen up. I did not kill Jamis. I didn't know him until I was accused of killing him. Someone wants to sully his name and mine. So far, it's working. But maybe together we can clear both our names. Will you work with me?"

He felt the tension in the man's body increase as he said, "Yeah, sure. I'll help you."

BB sighed. He didn't let go. "You're lying. But if someone killed my best friend, I'd probably go for revenge, too." He continued his hold on the man. "What's your name?"

"Ernest."

"Who hated Jamis? Who would spread a rumor about him?"

"No one hated him. Everyone liked him. He was—"

"—a great guy. You're not helping. Think. Someone spread a vicious rumor. That speaks of hate." *Unless his death had been a convenient ploy to smear my name.*

No. They could have put out I was a drug dealer and not implicated Jamis. "Think hard. Who told you about his death?"

"I heard it from his roommate."

"Who heard it from?" BB's arms ached. He shifted his weight to apply less force to the hold. He sensed the tension easing in his prisoner. It could be a ruse. BB stayed on guard. "Who told him?"

"I don't know. Probably school security."

"No. They would have told him Jamis died, but not he'd been dealing drugs, and certainly wouldn't have given my name as being involved."

The man relaxed in BB's hold. "I'm ready to listen."

BB unclamped his hands from behind his attacker's head. He dropped the shoulder hold and stepped back. He stayed on the balls of his feet in case Ernest decided to swing again.

He didn't. He dropped to the pavement and sat. BB joined him. Ernest stared at BB. "I never thought to ask where he heard about Jamis. I just assumed the police told him."

"What's the roommate's name?"

Ernest shook his head. "I'm not telling you."

"Then can we go together to talk to him? I've got my whole future riding on finding out who spread the lies about both of us. I want to know where they came from."

Ernest held up his hand. "I'm going for my phone."

BB waited. Ernest punched in a number. "Yeah. It's Ernest. Where did you hear about Jamis? No, man, it matters. Who told you he'd been killed?"

Silence followed. After a moment, Ernest nodded. "I see. Yeah. No, I figured the campus police told you. You don't know where she heard it from, do you?" Ernest's voice became heated. "Because someone is spreading rumors he was dealing drugs, and that's not the legacy Jamis deserves. So, ask her. And call me back."

He disconnected the call. "Heard it from his girlfriend."

BB groaned. "We're going to be here all night." He inhaled. "If that's what it takes."

Ernest stared at BB. "You really didn't kill him, did

you?"

"No, I didn't." BB didn't add no one did. It wasn't his calling to disparage the young man's name or Ernest's memory of him. All he had was Vic's word for Jamis' cause of death. But the way Vic had delivered it, BB had no reason to doubt his information. He, at least, had heard it from the police. Hadn't he? Or could that be another rumor?

Ernest's phone rang. No fancy tone, just an old-fashioned phone ringer. He answered it. "Yeah. From who? Who is she? What does she know about Jamis? Who did she hear it from?"

Frustration colored Ernest's tone. "Well, find out. Track it back as far as you can. Someone started this rumor. I want to know who. And I want to know tonight. Don't care. Don't care about that, either. This is for Jamis. He deserves better. Do it."

He hung up again. Ernest studied BB for a minute. "What's your name?"

"BB Andres." BB stuck out his hand.

The man did the same. "Ernest Conner."

BB asked, "Who pointed me out to you? If you didn't know me, who told you to attack me?"

Ernest stared at the ground. He looked up. "Friend of mine. He pointed you out at lunch. You were walking across the campus like you'd done nothing. He said you were the one who killed Jamis."

BB shook his head. "Does it do any good to ask where *he* heard it?"

Ernest tapped in a number on his phone. "Yeah. Need to know something. This afternoon, you showed me the guy who killed Jamis. How'd you know him? Heard it from where? Because I'm sitting here with the guy, and I tried to attack him. And he had nothing to do with Jamis. So, tell me who ID'd him to you."

"No, I don't need you to come out and help me." BB watched his fellow student roll his eyes. "I need you to help

Jamis by telling me how you knew he was the guy. Who told you? And how did they know? Someone on this campus has been spreading rumors, and I want to know where they started." He waited. "Well, find out. And call me back."

Ernest shook his head. "I am sorry. This is pathetic."

BB nodded. "It would be if lives weren't being affected by it. He heard it from someone who heard it from someone else, right?"

"Yeah." The man shifted on the ground. "This is getting cold. I apologize for hitting you from behind."

BB threw his hands in the air. "No harm, no foul for the attack."

"You're not going to report this?" Ernest sounded incredulous. But also grateful.

"No. You're trying to help me. That's all I care about."

"Fine. Give me your cell number. I'll call you when I hear from the others. And I promise I will track this down."

BB stuck out his hand again. "Thanks. I do appreciate it. Jamis deserves better."

Ernest shook his hand. "How did you know Jamis?"

"I didn't. But no one should have their name dragged in the gutter, and they can't defend themselves." Even when they could. But that didn't matter right now. BB gave William his contact information. The two men helped each other to their feet.

The man stepped away, then called over his shoulder, "I'll call you."

"Thanks." BB turned and walked toward the dorm. He paid closer attention to his surroundings and who might be lurking around. He saw no suspicious stalkers. His neck throbbed. He needed ice and a place to lie down.

He needed to call the dorm. Make sure the room had been cleared of smoke and partygoers. He texted Vic. *I'm coming up. Be there in ten minutes.*

Come now. No waiting.

Thanks. Be there in five.

BB doubled his pace across the parking lot, then slowed down. Moving too fast hurt his neck. He could feel the lump growing. And the stiffness setting in. Ah, well, it would work itself out. He tried rotating his shoulder but stopped. Not ready for that kind of pain. He held his shoulder with his hand and rode the elevator up to his floor.

The door to the room stood open. No music blared. Nice change. Maybe everyone was studying. Finals were coming. BB walked in the door.

It smelled like burned popcorn. And stale pizza. Studying had been going on. Vic sat at his desk, focused on his schoolwork. At least that's what it looked like. Samuel lounged on his bunk, headphones on, jamming to something only he would hear. Leeland sat at his desk, head down, maybe asleep. Maybe deep in concentration. More likely asleep.

BB walked to his dresser, pulled out a small towel, then walked to the fridge. He dumped ice out, wrapped it in the towel, and applied it to his shoulder.

Vic looked up. "What's with the shoulder?"

BB took a seat at his desk. "A guy attacked me for killing Jamis Fenton. We talked. He no longer thinks I'm a killer."

Vic's head jerked around. Leeland's head popped up from his desk. Samuel continued in his sound bubble. Vic barked, "Someone what? Attacked you?"

BB nodded, still holding the ice pack in place. "Yeah. Misunderstanding. He'd been told I was the drug dealer who knocked off Jamis for his territory. He objected to the insult to Jamis' memory and wanted me to know about it."

Vic's eyes narrowed. "So what? He knocks you in the head, then you two sit down and rationally discuss how he might have been wrong?"

BB dipped his head rather than shrug. "He took a little persuading. But he agreed I didn't do it. He's trying to track down who started the rumors. If we can do that, we can clear

Jamis' name from being a drug dealer and maybe mine for being a killer."

He saw pain in Vic's eyes. Leeland had a few comments BB refused to acknowledge, the gist of which became, "No way, dude." Vic stood and grabbed Samuel by the shoulder. The lineman sat, pulled off his headphones, and yelled, "What?"

"BB got knocked in the head for killing Jamis Fenton."

Samuel shook his head in disgust. "This is out of hand."

That wasn't exactly how he put it, but close enough for BB to interpret. Samuel continued, "Someone's got to can these rumors before someone else gets killed." He studied BB. "You okay?"

"Yeah. Got me in the neck."

Vic's voice dripped sarcasm. "Then they calmly sat and discussed it like gentlemen, of course."

BB scowled. "I said it wasn't like that. I had to take him down first. Once I got him in a hold he couldn't get out of, I made him listen to me. Then we had a calm discussion."

"How's he tracking down rumors?"

"Backtracking. Who told the person who told him? And on and on."

Samuel jumped off his bunk and laid his earphones on his desk. "You think you'll find a source of a rumor this size?"

"All rivers have a source." Even this one. Getting back to it might take a while, but every river head could be found sooner or later.

Vic pulled out his phone. He pointed to Leeland and Samuel. "Call whoever you heard it from. We need to stop this."

Samuel stared at the floor, then at the window, then at the desk. Finally, he pulled out his cell phone and texted someone.

Leeland did the same thing. BB massaged the ice onto his shoulder. "Leeland, who did you tell about me paying off your debt?"

Leeland shook his head. "No one, man. I didn't tell a soul. Not something I want to brag about."

BB swallowed that one. Gratitude might make one want to tell everyone, but then, there would have to be an admission of guilt first. Not likely in this case.

Vic lowered his eyes. "I may have sounded off to Carina."

Samuel groaned. "That's like telling the whole student body." He tossed his phone on his desk. "What exactly did you tell her?"

Vic raised both hands and held them in front of himself. "Only that BB bought Leeland from me. Lost me my best servant. I never said anything about killing Jamis. Never entered my mind. I didn't even know at the time it was Jamis who ki…who died." He stuttered over the words.

BB agreed. "Yeah, a few days passed before we learned who died." He cocked his head and studied Vic. "Though you said it had been someone in the dorm. Who told you?"

Vic scratched the back of his neck. "Someone on the team. Lancer, maybe? He heard it from one of the coaches."

BB numbered on his fingers. "We've got the story about a dead student. Then, the student is a drug dealer who someone killed to take over his territory. Then, I'm the killer."

Samuel tapped his hand on the desk. "Rumors get wider, not narrower. This one seems to target you."

Vic asked, "Who'd you insult? Snub? Make mad?"

BB shook his head. "No one. No one I can think of."

Leeland chewed the inside of his cheek. "You did stiff Riley Crimmons."

BB sat back in his chair. "I didn't stiff her. I told her I wouldn't come to her party."

Both Samuel and Vic made "Ohhhh" sounds. BB looked from one to the other. "What?"

Samuel nodded. "That explains it." He shoved his

headphones across the desk.

BB felt lost. "Explains what?" He massaged the ice harder into the aching muscle.

Vic shook his head slowly. "Woman scorned, man. Woman scorned. You don't refuse an invite from the most powerful woman on campus."

"She's what?" BB's tone came out incredulous. Matched his mood. He leaned forward to get a better look at Vic.

Vic pointed at BB's chest. "You, my friend, have committed two cardinal sins in the college world. First, you didn't know who you were dealing with. And second, you dealt her wrong. Riley Crimmons is the center of the women's world here. She is head of the Beta Kappa sorority. Any woman who wants to be anybody prominent has to go through Riley. She makes and breaks more people before breakfast than the Mafia does in a month."

BB scowled. "You're joking. No one is that powerful."

"Riley is. If you dissed her invite, she will stop at nothing to destroy you."

"But who am I to her?" BB threw up his hands. "I'm a nobody."

"Who she wanted to make into somebody. Who knows why she picks who she does? What matters is she picked you. And you snubbed her. She will be gunning for you the remainder of your college career. I'd think about switching colleges, man."

BB looked at Samuel. "He's lying, right?"

Samuel shook his head. "Not about this. Riley Crimmons is serious business."

BB's eyes widened. "What do I do?" Panic ate at the edges of his confidence.

Vic pulled out a bottle of Red Mike's Whiskey and poured some into a plastic cup. He raised it in a toast. "Here's to BB's demise. It's over. You're toast."

Samuel took the bottle and poured some for himself. He

swigged the shot. "Burned toast at that." He twisted his face at the liquor.

Leeland grabbed the whiskey and drank straight from the bottle. "Sorry for your luck, man. Nice knowing you."

BB glared at his roommates. "I'm glad you all think this is so funny."

Vic grimaced as the alcohol went down. His voice caught. "Not funny. Dead serious. Starting these rumors is just one of the ways she'll try to bury you."

BB inhaled, held his breath, then exhaled to a measured count of five. Calm returned to his senses. "Say she did start the rumors. Which ones? That Jamis could be a drug dealer? What would she have against him?"

Vic stopped in mid-word. He studied BB for a moment. "Good question. Why would she? Everyone liked Jamis. He was a regular guy."

Vic's eyes held BB's. BB read the warning. He protested, "I'm a regular guy."

Samuel interjected, "Who she singled out for attention. Let's get back to Jamis. Ruining him isn't her style."

But ruining me is? How twisted is her mind?

BB tried another tack. "If it wasn't Riley, then who else?"

Samuel offered, "It would have to be someone who didn't know Jamis. Not personally. They might have heard he died and thought this would be a perfect time to pin something on you."

"Not Riley, but someone working for Riley? Someone new?" An uncomfortable feeling flooded through BB. Julie said she didn't know anything about where the rumors came from. But she knew about Leeland...

BB went still inside. Lord? Please open my eyes. Help me see the truth. I don't want to accuse someone innocent. But I don't want to be blindsided by the enemy, either. Guide me, Father.

He looked at his roommates. "I want to wait and see if

we get any information on the genesis of the rumor mill. Then I can decide what to do." *What You want me to do, Lord. This is all in Your hands. I trust You to do Your will. Whatever happens.*

* * *

MONDAY AFTERNOON

Ben walked through the door and dropped his books on the wooden kitchen table. He would put them away later. Now, he needed to talk to his dad. And Wendy. His mom. He should call her that instead of Wendy. He should.

He walked into the living room and found Wendy reading a book. She looked up and smiled. "How was school?"

Ben's cheeks burned. "A girl kissed me."

Wendy's eyes opened wide. "She did? What girl?"

"Tricia. She kissed me on the cheek and said I was her only real friend. All her other friends want something from her. I'm the only one who doesn't, she said."

Wendy nodded. "I see. And what brought all this on?"

"Is Dad here?" Ben needed to talk to both of them. He couldn't take not saying something about the fight. His stomach continued to be in knots. He couldn't rest. He needed to tell Dad and Mom. They would know what to do.

Wendy motioned over her shoulder. "He's in the backyard fighting with the oleanders. He wants them out, but they are determined to stay."

Dad had been fighting with the bushes since they bought the house. Something about getting under the foundation.

Ben went to the back door and called, "Dad? Can you come in for a moment?"

Dad dropped the axe deep into the dirt. "For you, always, buddy."

Would Dad still call him 'buddy' when he knew Ben hid the truth? Would he still love him?

Dad grabbed a glass of ice water from the kitchen and sat across from Wendy. Sweat dripped down his forehead. He wiped it with the back of his sleeve. "I should have attacked those in the fall. They're full of sap now and tough as concrete."

Wendy laughed. "We didn't own this house in the fall, remember?"

"Oh, right. Right." Dad chuckled. "Time flies. What can we help you with, Ben?"

Ben stared at the floor. "Is it ever right to break a promise?"

Dad and Wendy exchanged looks. Dad's voice became quiet as he asked, "What kind of promise?"

"Tricia made me promise not to tell something. About the fight with Craig. She's afraid I'll be kicked out of school, and she'll lose her only friend. Me."

Dad's eyes looked gentle. That was good. He wasn't mad. You could tell when he was mad. His eyes burned. But he wasn't mad. Yet.

"Tell me about the fight. What happened to make Tricia think you'll get kicked out?"

Ben hung his head. "Craig said mean things about BB. Said he'd been accused of being a murderer and a drug dealer. I got mad and pushed him. He tried to hit me. I moved aside, and he hit the wall with his hand." Ben looked up. Tears filled his eyes. He brushed them with the back of his hand. "I'm sorry, Dad. I shouldn't have pushed him."

Dad came over and put a hand on Ben's shoulder. "No, you shouldn't have. But the principal would know this, right?"

Ben shook his head. "No. When we went to the principal's office, Tricia said Craig had started it. She didn't tell him about me shoving Craig." He bit his lip. "It's eating me. I didn't lie. I just didn't tell the whole truth." He sniffled. "Do you think I'll be kicked out of school like Craig?"

Dad squeezed his shoulder. "If you go to the principal and tell him the whole truth, you won't get kicked out. Not like Craig. Craig has been in trouble many times, and trying to hit you for whatever reason was the last straw. You've been a good student and haven't caused any trouble. I think you'll be fine. I'll go with you to talk to him if you want me to."

Ben looked at his feet. "No. I should go alone." He raised his head. "But you can come to school and wait outside the door."

Dad smiled. "I can do that."

Wendy said, "You asked about breaking a promise. Promises are dangerous things. We can make them over silly things like not telling someone what we got them for Christmas or their birthday. Or about going on trips. All things that will be told eventually. Do you understand? But if someone tells you never to share a secret, that's dangerous. Those are bad promises."

Ben nodded. "I understand. I won't make any bad promises." He stopped, then added, "Or ask anyone to make a bad promise for me. Right?"

Dad nodded. "Right." He smiled. "Do your homework, then come tackle the bushes with me. We'll pull out the bad roots together."

Ben went to his room and sat down at his desk. His first assignment was to write in his journal. He wrote, "DO NOT READ" across the top. Then he scrawled, *Today was the worst day ever. And the best day ever. It was the worst because I knew I'd done something wrong, and I lied about it. Well, I didn't lie. I just didn't tell the truth. And that's the same thing. I might get kicked out of school. Dad says I might not. I'll know tomorrow or whenever I can talk to the principal. I want to tell him the truth. I felt terrible about not telling Dad and Mom about it. It was the worst feeling of my life. But now that I told them, I feel better. I'm still scared that I'll get kicked out of school like Craig did, but I'll accept my punishment. BB is standing strong. I can, too.*

The good part is Tricia kissed me! She said I was her only friend. I'm not, but she says I am. I've never had a girl kiss me before. Not a real girl. Not a girl my age. I wonder if I'm falling in love? People talk about it all the time. Is this what it feels like? Am I old enough? I should ask Dad. Or BB. Except BB is having trouble with his girlfriend. I'll ask Dad.

He signed the page, "Ben(efactor) Andres. He liked using his old name. But only when no one would read it. No chance he'd be teased. He didn't need to give anyone more chances to tease him about being different. Even if Tricia thought his different was good. And she kissed him.

TUESDAY

Ben sat in the front of the bus, behind the driver. It was his favorite spot. He didn't get harassed by the older boys when he sat there. He'd learned that lesson quick. He'd sat in the rear the first time he took the bus. He didn't know it was reserved for the eighth graders. Or so they told him, when they picked on him and made fun of him. Even when he moved to the middle, the razing didn't stop. Only when he moved to be behind the driver did they stop their sneering.

Today, he sat in his regular place. His stomach hurt with the idea that he was going to have to ask to see the principal. Dad said he should go in first thing and tell the office he needed to see Mr. Hardaway. There would be all the questions. Why do you want to see him? What's this about? Can it wait? Can it wait until after school? Or tomorrow?

What if Mr. Hardaway wasn't there today? What if he had to live with this feeling in his stomach for a whole 'nother day and night? Could he stand it?

Of course, BB was living with the rumors about him all the time. And they weren't his fault. This *was* Ben's fault. He would be brave like BB. And suck it up.

A voice from the back of the bus yelled, "Hey, Andres! I heard you got Craig kicked out of school."

Ben didn't answer. The driver looked in the rearview mirror but said nothing.

Someone else hissed, "You'll get yours, you little

punk." Voices joined in jeering and sneering.

The driver looked in the mirror again. "Let's keep it down. I see each of you." He paused, then added, "I know all of you. Cameras are on. Remember that." He caught Ben's eye in the mirror. "I'll keep a look out."

Ben nodded. "Thanks." He didn't need the bus driver's help, did he? He had Jesus. That should be enough. Jesus said He would watch over His sheep. Ben was one of His sheep. He didn't have anything to be afraid of.

He climbed off the bus as soon as it stopped and hurried to the office. He had to wait in line with students turning in notes, getting notes, getting new bus assignments, or looking for the lost and found. Finally, it was his turn. He stepped up to the receptionist. "I need to speak to Mr. Hardaway."

She smiled. "What's this about?"

Ben had practiced his answer. Over and over. Why couldn't he remember it now? His heart thumped in his chest. His palms felt sweaty. His voice tremored. "I want to talk to him about the fight with Craig."

The woman looked at a piece of paper. "I'm sorry. He's going to be gone until eighth period. You could speak to him after school. Or wait until tomorrow. He'll have time in the morning."

Ben swallowed hard. "I'll see him after school. I ride the bus home, but I can call my dad and tell him to pick me up."

She nodded. "Very well. I'll put you down for 4:30. Your name, please?"

"Ben Andres."

She wrote it down. "Fine. Mr. Hardaway will see you today at 4:30. You can call your parent before school starts."

Ben moved to a corner of the office. It would be quieter than out in the halls. He punched in the home number.

Dad picked up. "Done so soon?"

"I need a ride home tonight. I can't see Mr. Hardaway until after school. The secretary said it would be 4:30 when he could see me. Would you pick me up then?"

Dad's voice sounded even. "Sure thing, bud. I'll leave here then and pick you up around five."

Ben thought hard. "The school grounds will be closed at five. I'll meet you across the street at the city bus stop."

"Good thinking. I'll see you then. You're not alone, Ben."

"I know. Jesus is with me."

"Yes, He is."

"Bye." Ben hung up. He didn't really need Dad to remind him Jesus was with him. But it was nice to hear.

The rest of the day felt forever long. He was "bumped into" three times in the hall. Twice, he had his books knocked out of his hands. Once he was bounced off the wall. Always, the offender would apologize. "Oh, I'm sorry. Did I do that?" And then they'd laugh.

Ben took it. He knew it was because of Craig. All the ones who knocked into him were Craig's friends. But it always looked like an accident. Nothing Ben could report as targeting him. But he kept it in mind. Always in mind. He would tell Mr. Hardaway about it. Maybe they would get suspended, too.

As he sat at lunch, he thought about it. Where did it end? If he said something, then that would make them even madder, and they'd do something else. But should they be allowed to get away with pushing him around? With pushing anyone around? Maybe he should push back.

Was that what Jesus would do?

Ben mulled it over the remainder of his day. He thought he knew what Jesus would do. What BB was doing. Taking the insult. Turning the other cheek, Dad called it. But did that mean letting them push him around without saying anything at all?

He sat in the office from the time class let out until it was time for his appointment with the principal. At least in the office, no one would shove him into the lockers. Finally,

Principal Hardaway called his name. Ben stepped into the room. The principal motioned to the chair beside him. "What can I do for you, Mr. Andres?"

Ben sat and lifted his head as Dad had told him. He looked Mr. Hardaway in the eyes. "I want to tell you what happened when Craig tried to hit me. What led up to the incident."

Mr. Hardaway raised his eyebrows. "Oh? There is more to the story?"

Ben nodded. "Tricia told you Craig started the fight by swinging at me. She only told you part of the truth." Ben swallowed hard but kept his head straight. "Craig made accusations against my brother. False accusations. He called him a drug dealer and a murderer." Ben pushed forward. "I didn't like it, and I shoved Craig. That's when he tried to hit me, and I moved aside. He hit the wall instead of me."

The principal tapped a pencil against his desktop. He eyed Ben closely. "You shoved him?"

"Yes, I did." Dad's voice echoed in his mind. "Don't try to excuse it. Just state the facts. If he asks if you're sorry, tell him the truth. Be honest. Jesus said the truth will set you free. Live it."

Mr. Hardaway stared at the floor. "You didn't say anything about this when it happened, did you?"

Ben squared his shoulders. "No, sir, I did not. I was shocked by Craig's hand, and the blood and all. Then Tricia jumped in and said what happened. I didn't realize she'd left out the part about me shoving Craig until the next day." Ben looked at the floor. "I felt miserable all day. I realized not telling the whole truth is the same as lying. I don't want to be a liar."

Mr. Hardaway nodded. "You came to an important realization, Mr. Andres. I'm glad you learned it. What did your parents have to say?"

Again, Ben squared his shoulders and lifted his head. "They said I would be right to tell you about it. And we would take whatever consequence you feel is right." Ben studied Mr. Hardaway's face. "I hope you let me stay in school and don't expel me. I'm sorry I didn't say something sooner."

"I can see you're sorry. The fact you came in at all says it bothered you. I'm proud of you for coming forward." He sighed. "But we have very strict policies about fighting. You won't be expelled. Craig was a special case. He has been on notice for behavioral problems, and swinging at you proved to be his last offense. You've never been in trouble before. By all accounts, you're a very good student. Your grades are above average. Your teachers always have positive things to say about you. So, I will give you the minimum sentence. You'll be suspended for three days. Since Friday is a holiday, you'll only miss two days of actual school."

Ben closed his eyes. Popdad Quinn's voice spilled into his mind. *"Take punishment like Jesus did. He didn't talk back. No whining. No complaining. Say, 'Thank you' and go on."*

Ben opened his eyes. "Thank you for not expelling me. Will I be able to make up the lessons I miss?"

Mr. Hardaway nodded. "I think we can allow it. Normally we don't. But I think you've learned your lesson. Are you sorry?"

Ben breathed in and out. "I'm sorry I reacted the way I did. I should not have pushed Craig."

The principal smiled. "That's as honest a statement as I'm going to hear today. Okay, Ben. You can gather your things and go home. I appreciate you coming in like this." He stood.

Ben followed suit. He extended his hand to shake Mr. Hardaway's. "Thank you, sir, for listening to me. And not expelling me."

"Have a good day, Ben."

Ben turned and walked out of the office. He felt light. Lighter than he'd felt in days. He'd told the truth. And he hadn't been kicked out of school. Suspended for three days. But only two school days. He went to his locker for his books and notes. He would take them all home. And make sure he opened them while he was there. And did the work.

Ben left the fenced area before it was locked for the evening. He crossed the street to the city bus stop and sat down. It wasn't five yet. Dad would come soon. He was always on time. He said he'd rather be ten minutes early than five minutes late. Wendy wasn't quite that on time. But she tried.

Ben saw the trouble coming down the street. Three of Craig's friends were bouncing a basketball, walking on the other side of the block. They were headed in his direction. As long as they stayed on their side, he would be safe. And not worry. He whispered, "When I get afraid, I trust in You, Lord." Not that he was afraid. No. Jesus was with him. He would be fine.

He looked down at his bookbag and moved it closer to his feet. A voice yelled, "Hey, loser!"

Ben looked up in time to see a basketball inches from his face. The impact knocked his head backward and brought tears to his eyes. He leaned over on the bench to catch his breath.

The boys were on him. They punched him, dragged him off the bench, then kicked him in the knees and stomach. One of them stomped down on his leg. Ben didn't make a sound. He went back to his days in the hills when if you cried, they beat you harder. He curled into a ball and tried to protect his head. All the while, the boys kept yelling and jeering and cursing at him.

Mr. Hardaway's voice bellowed, "Stop! Get away from him!"

A car screeched to a halt. Dad yelled, "Hey! Leave him alone!"

Ben heard footsteps running in different directions. Dad kneeled beside him. "I'm here, Ben. I'm here. Don't move."

Ben could taste blood in his mouth. He tried to sit, but Dad told him, "Just stay down." That seemed like a really good idea. He heard Dad speaking into his phone, "I need an ambulance at the corner of Seventh and Wolf."

Ambulance? Ben wanted to protest. But it hurt to move. Maybe an ambulance would be a good thing. He lay still. Dad carefully squeezed along Ben's legs and arms. Maybe he was checking for broken bones? They didn't feel like they were broken. But he'd never had one and didn't know what it would feel like.

Until Dad touched his shoulder. Ben cried out in pain. Dad let go. "I'm sorry, Ben. I'm sorry." Dad didn't try to move anything else. He did wipe blood from Ben's mouth. Ben could feel his lips swelling. Dad covered Ben with his jacket and paced around the area. He made calls to the Knights. "Tav. Ben's been beaten up. Yeah. I'm waiting for the ambulance. If I weren't afraid there might be something internal, I'd take him in myself. Yeah. Activate the tree. But I'll call Wendy. Right."

"Wendy. No, I've got him. But three boys beat him up. No, stay at the house until we get him to the hospital. I don't know. I don't want to take chances. They had him on the ground kicking him. Right. I'll call you."

Dad's phone pinged. "Yeah. I'm the one who called. I'm standing right here with my son. He's been attacked by three boys, ages probably thirteen or fourteen. They had him on the ground…right. Please hurry. He's got at least a possible broken shoulder. I don't know what else. Right. I'll be here."

Dad sat on the ground beside Ben. He laid his hand on Ben's head. "I'm so sorry, son. I'm so sorry."

Ben's chest hurt. He wanted to ask what Dad was sorry about, but he didn't want to talk either. He'd wait until the ambulance came and made him feel better.

Dad began talking to Jesus. "Why, Lord? Why my son? Why now? Aren't we being tested enough with BB? You know what's in my heart. You know I love you. Why this?"

He sounded upset. Heartbroken. It didn't make sense. Ben loved Jesus. Jesus loved Ben. Yes, Ben knew there were reasons he didn't understand. God was God. He could do what he wanted. But why did Ben have to hurt? Why did the bad guys win?

Mr. Hardaway sounded out of breath. "I didn't catch them, but I saw who they were. And I know them. I'll tell the police."

He heard sirens in the distance. He closed his eyes and wished they would hurry up. Lots of places were hurting. Everywhere.

Dad urged him, "Stay awake, Ben. Don't close your eyes. Not yet."

Ben muttered, "But it hurts."

"Talk to me. Does your head hurt?"

"No. Everything else does."

"I know, buddy. They're coming. We'll get you to the hospital and get you checked out. But you have to stay awake for me. Can you do that?"

Ben didn't nod. It hurt to nod. He muttered, "I'll stay awake."

"Good job, son."

Ben saw the red paramedic squad roll to a stop. He didn't look up but watched as booted feet in uniform pants approached him. A man kneeled beside him. "Hey, man. How are you doing?"

Ben could hear Dad talking to someone. But he focused on the man beside him. "I hurt all over."

"I'm sure you do. My name's Walt. Can you tell me your name and what happened?"

"Ben. Three guys jumped me. They hit me with a basketball in the face, then knocked me down and kicked me."

"I see. Is there any place that hurts more than anywhere else?"

"My shoulder. My chest. My stomach."

Walt looked over his shoulder. "Bring the stretcher." He laid a hand on Ben's arm. "We're going to get some vitals, then we're going to transport you to the hospital, where we'll take some pictures of your insides and see if anything is broken."

Tears trickled down Ben's cheek. He sniffed. "Tell my dad to take care of my books and my book bag. It has my assignments in it."

Walt smiled. "You must like school."

Ben sighed. "Not this school. Except my teachers. And Tricia."

"Is she your girlfriend?" Walt put a blood pressure cuff on Ben's arm. The man moved Ben's arm as little as possible.

Ben grunted, "Sort of. But she's my friend."

"Best kind to have, Ben." Walt called, "One hundred over sixty-five. Pulse is 100."

Another medic put an oxygen line around Ben's face and under his nose. They put their hands under his shoulders and thighs. One of them counted to three, then they lifted him onto the stretcher.

Dad leaned into Ben's face. "They're going to take you to the hospital. I'll be right behind you. I'll call your mom and tell her to meet us there. You won't be alone."

For the first time, Ben's heart jumped. Alone. With Jesus he was never alone. But where was Jesus? He promised nothing would happen to His chosen ones. But this wasn't nothing. Was Jesus still with him?

"Dad? Is Jesus with me?"

Dad's voice cracked. "Yes, He is. He's with you. He'll never leave you."

It took too much energy to ask what he wanted. He nodded instead and kept the question to himself. He'd ask later. When he didn't hurt so bad.

Walt and his partner shoved the stretcher into the squad.

Walt climbed in the back with Ben. "I'll ride along with you. You're going to be just fine." Walt's partner slid into the driver's seat. He turned on the siren and drove down the street.

Walt asked Ben questions. "How old are you, Ben?"

"Thirteen."

"Do you have any allergies?"

"No."

"Have you ever been in the hospital before?"

"Maybe when I was born."

Walt chuckled. "Good answer. I'm going to ask you some questions that might seem silly but answer them anyhow. What day is it?"

Ben sighed.

* * *

It felt like hours, and probably was, before Ben was wheeled into a room of his own. He had an IV in his arm taped to a board so he wouldn't pull it out by accident. Like he'd do that. Dad and Mom waited for him as the bed made the turn through the doorway. His brain said, "Smile." His body said, "Forget it." Ben mumbled, "I want to go home."

Dad and Mom stood out of the way until the nurses were finished, then came up and kissed him. They were careful kisses, not "I'm so happy to see you" kisses. Like they thought he would break. Maybe he would if they touched him too hard. The doctors had treated him like he would. The worst part was they never told him what they found. Or didn't find.

The nurses left the room, but a doctor came in. He smiled at Ben. "I'm Doctor Knowles. Young man, your job is to rest tonight. I know you'd rather be in your own bed. But we want to keep you overnight to watch you and make sure there are no surprises we don't know about. If nothing comes up, we'll send you home in the morning."

He looked at Dad and Wendy and motioned with his head. "We can talk in the hall."

Dad said, "No. You can talk in front of our son. Ben understands and deserves to know. I trust him to follow what you're saying."

Ben's insides warmed. Dad trusted him. Dad thought he was grown-up enough to hear what was wrong. He would be strong like Dad thought he was.

The doctor shrugged. "As you wish. All our scans have shown evidence of trauma but not ruptures or tears to the internal organs. Plenty of bruising, as is expected after a beating like he took." Doctor Knowles shook his head. "I hope they catch the ones who did this." He breathed in, then continued, "The left clavicle appears to have sustained a fracture. We'll need to do an MRI to be certain. That can wait until tomorrow. The orthopedic people will make the determination and decide how to treat it."

Ben furrowed his brow. Clavicle? Did he remember what bone that was? Clavicle…clavicle…oh, right. The collarbone. Above the ribcage. No wonder his shoulder hurt when he moved it. He went back to listening.

Dad was asking questions. "…copies of all the records for the police report?"

"We'll make sure they're available."

Dad nodded. "Good. I want to be sure we have everything we need." Dad shook hands with Doctor Knowles. The doctor left the room, closing the door behind him.

Dad and Wendy stood on either side of his bed. Mom looked worn out. Dad looked concerned. Angry. And worn out. Dad pulled a chair up beside the bed for Mom. She sat but reached out to hold Ben's hand. Dad continued to stand. Ben looked up at him. Ben's eyes were swollen but he tried to focus anyhow. "Is BB here?"

"He's waiting in the hall. You can only have two visitors at a time. He'll be in before you go to sleep."

"Are you going to call the police?"

"I already have. Mr. Hardaway was leaving school and

saw the whole thing. He says he knows who the boys were that attacked you. The police rounded them up earlier this evening while you were still in X-ray having your CT scan."

Ben lowered his eyes. "Shouldn't we forgive them?"

Dad paused before answering. "Yes, we should. And we will. But being forgiven by us is different from being forgiven by the law. They still have to face the consequences of what they did. So they learn not to do it to someone else."

Ben had to think that one over. He waited, then asked, "Does Jesus make us face the consequences when He forgives us?"

"Sometimes. Sometimes He removes the penalty. He removed the penalty when we sinned against God. But in that instance, He took the penalty away from us and put it on Himself. He paid the consequence."

Ben thought again. "Am I paying the penalty for my sin? Did I do something to deserve this?"

Dad and Wendy both reached and hugged him. Carefully. "No, Ben. No. You did nothing wrong. Nothing. You're not paying for anything you did. You're hurting because of what those boys did."

Mom kissed him on the head. "We can talk when you're feeling better. Right now, you need to rest. Sleep if you can. Your dad and I will be right here if you need anything. The nurses left you the call button. I'll slip out after we pray and let BB come in for a moment." She held him in her eyes. "You're not to get out of bed without calling for help. Understand? Not for any reason."

Ben grimaced. "But what if—"

"Not for any reason. You push the call button if you need anything. Anything. You understand?"

Ben grumbled, "Yes, Mom."

Dad looked at the closed door. "I sent the rest of the Knights home. They were all here at first. Once the doctors said they didn't find anything critical, they went home. But they are all praying for you. Jen said to tell you since she's up all night with the twins, she'll pray for you through the night."

Dad and Wendy joined hands across Ben's bed. Dad prayed, "Lord, we don't understand why You allowed this." Ben noted a bit of anger still in Dad's voice. Could Dad be mad at God? Could anyone be mad at God? He'd have to ask. Tomorrow.

Dad continued, "But we know two things. You are God. You are in control. And all You do is good. Be with Ben tonight. Take away his pain and heal his body. Lord, Your will is what matters. Let it be done. In Jesus' Name, amen."

The prayer warmed him. Like a hug. Or a blanket. Wendy slipped out of the door, and BB came in. His face looked hollow and dark like Dad and Mom's. Ben tried to smile, but his face didn't move. He said instead, "Hey, BB."

BB leaned in and kissed him on the side of the head. He acted like Ben would break, too. Was everyone going to act like that? The doctor said he was going to be okay. Didn't anyone believe Doctor Knowles?

BB laid his hand on Ben's good shoulder. "I'm so sorry, Ben. This is my fault."

Ben interrupted him. "Don't say that. It's not. The boys wanted to hurt me because of Craig, not because of you."

BB shook his head. "But Craig got expelled because of the rumors about me."

Dad cut him off. "Craig was expelled for his own deeds. The boys who beat Ben are responsible for theirs. You are not the cause of this in any way, shape, or form. No more talk about whose fault any of this is. Got it? We're done." There was an anger in Dad's voice that seemed out of place. But maybe he was tired, too. Sometimes, when Dad was tired, he said things differently. And then had to apologize after. Was this one of those times?

Ben tapped his knuckles on BB's. "Right. No more." BB smiled. He still looked tired. Dad said, "I think we should let Ben get some sleep. BB, send Wendy back in. You go home and rest. We'll take the first watch. And call you in the morning to let you know what the doctor says about Ben going home."

BB nodded. "Hang in there, little brother."

Ben nodded. He was growing more and more sleepy by the moment. BB walked out and Wendy came back. She sat down in the chair beside him. "Go to sleep, Ben."

"Yes, Mom." Ben closed his eyes and let the world slip away.

* * *

WEDNESDAY MORNING

BB raged in the room. "They hurt my little brother! They beat him and put him in the hospital." He paced back and forth. "I want to know where that rumor came from! I want to track it down to its source and find out who started it."

Vic, Samuel, and Leeland all nodded. Vic shook his head. "I've done some low stuff in my time, but getting a kid hurt? That's beyond low."

Samuel questioned, "Do they know who did it?"

BB breathed in, trying to regain composure. He had none. All he could see was the form of his brother lying in that bed, battered, bruised, cut, swollen…and trying to smile at him. Knowing Ben would be okay and might go home that afternoon did nothing to ease BB's pain. His brain kept repeating, *This is your fault. This is your fault.* How didn't matter. He hadn't protected Ben. That was his job. His duty. And he failed.

Leeland held up his phone. "It's on the news. Three juveniles are being held in connection with an assault across from the middle school yesterday afternoon. Names withheld due to the ages of the assailants. But one was sixteen. He could be transferred to adult court."

BB's insides went cold. "They nearly killed him. They

wanted to kill him. If someone hadn't stopped them, they would have. They beat him like a dog." Tears burned in his eyes. His fists clenched. His body shook. All the emotions he had bottled this morning when he saw Ben were coming out. And they were anything but godly.

He screamed in fury. "AARRGGHH!!" Then he dropped to his chair and collapsed.

No one said anything for several moments. Vic broke the silence. "You gonna be okay, bro?"

BB calmed his breathing. It took several breaths…several long, deep breaths…to get himself under control. But he lifted his head. "Yeah. I'm sorry."

Samuel shook his head. "I'd be furious, too, if I had a little brother and someone did that to him."

BB stared at his desk. "I have to find out who started these rumors. Have to." He looked at his roommates. "Will you help?"

"What do you want us to do?" Vic cocked his head to stare at BB.

"Trace them back. We've all got to call and keep calling."

"Can do." Vic pulled out his phone and began dialing.

BB didn't question his roommate's willingness to help. He accepted it for the help it was. And accepted it gratefully. Samuel and Leeland began making calls as well. They would get to the bottom…or top…of this. Somehow.

* * *

It was a silent drive home from the hospital. Dad seemed subdued. Quiet. The doctor had said Ben would be fine. He needed to rest. They would have an appointment next week to talk about the collarbone. For now, his shoulder had been immobilized. And he had pain pills to take. They'd given him a shot for the ride home, but it would wear off in another hour or so. Ben wanted to be brave like his dad was when he was in pain. Dad didn't take pain pills. Ben wouldn't either.

Dad asked him, "I never asked what Mr. Hardaway said when you met with him. How did that go?"

"He didn't kick me out. He said I had been honest. I'm suspended but can make up my work."

Dad nodded. "That's a great. You did good in there, then." He didn't ask questions or grill Ben about what might have been said. He accepted Ben told him the truth. Dad trusted Ben. It made a difference. It did. Ben nodded to himself. *I want to be like Dad. He wants to be like Jesus. So do I.*

Ben looked at Dad. "If I follow you, and you follow Jesus, will that make me like Jesus, too?"

Dad thought a moment, then his voice was serious. "Only if you follow the Jesus parts. Because I don't get it right all the time. Don't follow those parts. Matter of fact, just follow Jesus, not me. That way, you'll be sure to get it right."

Ben tossed the thought around his head for several moments. "I think I see. But you're teaching me what Jesus said and did so I can follow those parts of you."

"Right. The Jesus parts. Not the Mick Andres parts that don't look like Jesus."

"Right." Ben pondered a moment. "How will I know which is which?"

Dad chuckled. "Ask your mother. She'll be more than able to tell you when I'm acting on my own. She's very good at knowing the difference." Mom sneered at Dad.

"Is that a good thing?" This sounded like one of those married people things.

Dad took a long breath. "Most of the time." He smiled. "Yes, it is. I need someone to remind me when I'm not acting like Jesus . It's why God gave us partners to help us."

Ben nodded. "I hope I have someone tell me someday."

"You will."

They arrived home, and Dad helped him into the house and to the living room, where Dad sat him in the big chair.

Wendy brought out a blanket and put it over and around him. Dad stood back and told him, "If you need anything, you ask for it. Don't try to get up on your own. Call one of us. All those muscles you bruised will make you very sore and won't want to cooperate. You'll be limping around for days. And that's okay. You have to take it easy."

"Would you take it easy?"

Wendy answered, and her voice was sharp. "Yes, because I wouldn't let him do anything else. That's one of those 'why God gave us partners' things. You're not to try to be like your father."

Dad's face looked sheepish. He put his hand on Ben's head. "Listen to your mom. She's right. Your body needs time to heal. It won't if you don't let the muscles ease back to the way they were. And yes, I take pain pills when I need them. That's something else I learned. So no trying to be a hero. If you hurt, say so. Got that?"

Ben nodded. "I will. I love you, Dad. I love you, Mom."

He saw tears in Dad's eyes. "Love you, son." Dad didn't try to hide how he felt. Maybe that was a good thing, too. Ben had a lot to learn about being an adult. But he had good parents who were going to help him. He knew that much. He settled back in the chair and closed his eyes.

* * *

WEDNESDAY EVENING

Tracking back the rumors to their start proved to be a long process. The further back it went, the more BB began to distrust the validity of who said what to who. And did it matter?

BB stared at the chart he and his roommates were building. It looked like a phone recall tree in reverse. They had all the lines feeding into the central trunk but no firm lead on the origin at the top.

Samuel took the sheet from BB and added a name. He stared at the tree. His eyes narrowed, and he pointed to the lists. "There's no split. Jamis has always been part of the rumor. Whoever started it deliberately involved Jamis. And they knew of his death before anyone official said anything."

BB muttered, "Like they were involved." His head snapped up. "Samuel…you think someone killed Jamis? Just to smear me? That's insane."

Vic came over to the desk. "What did you say? You still think someone killed Jamis? But the police found a note."

"Have they authenticated it? Do they know it came from him?"

Vic held BB's eyes. The man's face looked blank, almost in shock. "I don't know. I assumed…" He turned away and sat down on his bunk. Vic stared at the floor.

Samuel humphed. He shook his head. "I still don't understand. People liked Jamis. He had no enemies."

"That we know of. Could he have crossed someone?"

Samuel shook his head. "I don't see it."

Leeland came over from his desk. "No one ever does." He handed BB a piece of paper with names and numbers written on them. "Interesting information."

BB searched Leeland's eyes. "What?"

Leeland pointed to a group of names. "These all heard about Jamis dying."

BB waited. "So?" Half the campus knew about Jamis' death, seemingly within hours.

"Before Jamis died." Leeland pointed to the time he had written beside the names.

BB jerked his head up. "What?" He grabbed the paper in both hands and stared hard at what Leeland had written.

Samuel and Vic both jumped up and stared over Leeland's shoulder. "What?"

Leeland nodded. "Police say Jamis died about midnight. But these four all received the rumors before ten p.m."

BB exchanged glances with Vic. "Then Jamis *was* murdered."

Vic urged, "Who contacted them? Who started the rumor?" The intensity in his voice grew marked.

"That's the fuzzy part. None of the people I talked to will admit who they heard the rumor from. But they are certain of the time. Around ten." Leeland stepped back and raised his head.

BB looked around the room. "We need to call the police. We need to tell them what we've found." He zeroed in on Vic. "Jamis deserves this."

Vic nodded. His voice cut the air. "Someone tried to use him. Made it look like suicide, then changed it to I had been involved. I want them brought down." His eyes burned as hard as his voice.

BB nodded. "Right." He picked up his phone. "It's

going to be a long night."

Samuel moved to his desk and sat. "You can't call it in as an emergency. And the detectives who are on the case aren't going to come out tonight. Why don't we wait until tomorrow? We can all go together in the morning. Miss classes, I know. But this matters more."

Vic kicked the bed. "I hate waiting until tomorrow. I want this cleared up now."

BB tapped his desk. "Agreed. I want this over, as well. But Samuel's right. All the information will be there in the morning. And we can put it in some kind of form the police can use." Something other than the chicken scratches they had now.

Vic snorted. "That's your job, geek. You understand all that stuff." He moved to his desk and sat.

BB protested. "It's no different than your playbook. You have to see all the variables in there."

"Yeah, but the coach tells me which ones go with which."

Leeland pulled his chair up next to BB's. "I'll help. I kinda like doing spreadsheets."

BB raised his eyebrows. "You sure?" This would be a new side of Leeland no one had ever seen. At least not in this room.

Leeland nodded. "Yeah. I sort of understood where it was going. I'd like to learn more about the patterns." He began tracing the tree branches with his pencil.

Vic turned away. So did Samuel. BB waved at Leeland. "Let's do it."

The two men set to work.

An hour later, a call buzzed BB's phone. He looked at the number. Julie. Hmm. He answered it on speaker. "Hey."

"Hey yourself. What are you doing?"

"Working on a project with Leeland. What's up?"

"Thought you might join me for coffee? I've got something I need to discuss with you."

BB stared at the phone. He looked at his roommates. Vic shrugged. Samuel waved him off. Leeland whispered, "I've got this."

BB turned to the phone. "Sure. Where do you want to meet me?"

"My car's down. Can you pick me up?"

BB felt the nudge in his spirit but ignored it. He said, "Sure."

Vic shot up to attention and began waving "no" in the air. With vigor and purpose. BB said, "Hang on." He put the phone on mute.

Vic insisted, "Don't do it. Do not go alone with any woman at this time. If Riley is gunning for you, Julie could be part of the plan. You don't need any more trouble." Leeland and Samuel nodded.

The internal nudge grew to a full-on kick in the shins. BB unmuted his phone. "Sorry, Julie. I'm in the room, and Vic had something to say. It would be better if I meet you. I'll pay for your ride share."

"I'm not comfortable with ride-sharing. We've ridden together before. What's the problem?"

"It's late, it's after dark, and I don't want to compromise either of us. What if we meet at the cafeteria?" He looked at his roommates for agreement. Three heads nodded. Vic gave him a thumbs-up.

Sarcasm laced the young woman's voice. "Oh, great choice. We can have a nice conversation there."

Vic and Samuel both waved a "No-go" sign. BB nodded and told Julie, "I'm sorry, but that's the best we can do if you can't get a ride. What's wrong with the car?"

"How am I supposed to know? It's not running. Won't start. Something's wrong with it. I'm not a mechanic."

Vic pointed to himself and mouthed, "I am."

BB raised his eyebrows and then gave him a thumbs-up sign. "What if I bring a mechanic to look at it? For free?" Lots of revelations tonight.

"At this hour? Why would someone do that?"

"He's a friend." Vic nodded. His eyes sparked. He even smiled.

Exasperation filled her tone. "Fine. Just dandy. Meet me at the parking lot."

"See you in twenty minutes."

The phone went dead. BB punched in another number. "Campus security? There's a female student with a broken-down car. A friend and I are going to look at it, but being as it's this late, I'm sure she'd feel better if you were there with her when we get there. Julie Williams. Dorm 20. She drives a yellow four-door sedan. CA plates. 7AAA111. Right. We told her we'd be there in twenty minutes. I'm sure she'll appreciate the presence. Safety and all that. Yeah. Thanks."

Vic held out a fist. He grinned. "Smooth, man. Very smooth."

Samuel nodded. "Smart, too."

BB tapped his fists with Vic. "My dad didn't raise a dummy." *Okay, Lord, I wasn't listening. But thank You for using Vic to warn me. Protect us all, Father. And end this farce. Please.*

Vic and BB left Samuel and Leeland, walked to the parking lot, and got in BB's car. They drove to the parking lot of Dorm Twenty. It wasn't hard to find Julie. She had parked under a light. The young woman leaned against the front of her car, waiting for them. The driver's side door stood open, also waiting for them.

Julie looked at Vic, and her eyes narrowed. "You're the friend? The mechanic?"

Vic smirked. "A man of many talents. May I?" He pointed to the driver's seat.

Julie waved him in. "Go right ahead. Work some magic."

Vic turned the key in the ignition and received silence. Nothing. He looked at BB. "Battery's dead."

Julie scoffed. "I can guess that. Why is the battery

dead?"

Vic ignored her sarcasm and popped the hood from inside the car. BB lifted the hood and shone a flashlight on the battery.

One of the cables had been cut. The cable clamp was missing. Vic picked up the lead and taunted, "Well, there's your problem."

Julie stared hard at the useless lead. "How did that happen?"

BB's tone darkened. "Not by itself. Do you leave your car unlocked?"

"Never." Julie glared at him. "I'm not a dummy."

"Well, someone broke in without damaging the door or the window, popped the hood, then cut the end off the cable clamp and took it with them."

Julie's eyes widened. "They did what?"

Vic nodded his approval. "Slick trick, that, without having the keys. Wonder why just one clamp and not both?"

BB shrugged. "Maybe they only needed one?"

Julie crossed her arms over her chest. "I'm glad you two think this is amusing."

Campus Security pulled up in their cart. "Is there a problem here?" A young woman officer climbed out of her seat. BB read her name tag. Officer Dewars.

Julie said sharply, "No."

BB corrected, "Yes. Her car has been vandalized." Julie threw daggers with her eyes.

The officer shined her flashlight on Julie's engine area. Vic indicated the damaged battery cable. "Someone cut the end off."

Julie gave an exaggerated sigh. "It's probably a prank. Not a good one, but nothing critical. I can get it fixed."

BB shook his head. "What about someone breaking into your car? Did you check to see if anything had been stolen?"

Ms. Dewars pulled out a notebook. "A break-in? When did this happen?" She eyed Julie expectantly.

Julie protested. "No one said anyone broke into my car. They could have popped the hood from underneath." She pointed to the front of the engine compartment.

Vic smirked. "Not likely. That's why the manufacturers put the release on the inside. To prevent unauthorized entry." He turned to BB and nodded.

Julie gave an exaggerated sigh. "Fine. Someone broke into the car, lifted the hood, and cut the cable. I don't want to file a report, and I don't want to make a big deal out of this. I just want to get it fixed so I can drive."

Officer Dewars extracted a pen from her top pocket. "You might not care. But we have to report all damage to cars whether you file a claim or not." She smirked. "School policy. Insurance. Security has to justify our existence somehow."

Julie groaned and rolled her eyes. BB suggested, "I think I may have a spare in my trunk. Never leave home without backup parts." *Thank you, Dad.*

Vic tapped fists with BB. "Someone raised you right."

"Be prepared. That's our motto. That, and 'What would Jesus do?' But they kind of go together. He was prepared for everything."

Vic eyed BB sideways. "But He's God, so He already knew what He needed, right?"

BB dipped his head to the side. "True. But He's also human. Fully God and fully Man." He faced Vic. He might never get a better chance to explain the Incarnation than now.

Julie's voice carried more than a note of sarcasm. "Can we spare the theology lesson? And get to fixing my car?"

Officer Dewars asked, "Name?"

"Julie Williams. No, I don't know what time my car got broken into." She stuck her hands in the pockets of her jacket.

BB suggested, "But you knew it wasn't running. When did you figure that part out?"

If eyes could fry, BB would be ultra-crispy. Julie snarled, "At noon. I went to go to lunch off campus. The car wouldn't start. I didn't know it had been vandalized. I only knew it wouldn't start."

"And you didn't look under the hood?" Officer Dewars sounded surprised.

Julie mocked the officer's question. "No, I didn't look under the hood. I know nothing about car engines. I could tell you there's an engine installed, but that would be the sum of it."

"Was anything stolen from the vehicle?"

"No."

BB eyed Julie closely. She hadn't known there'd been a break-in. And she hadn't checked since learning about it. Interesting. He kept his musings to himself. This time.

BB pulled out his toolbox and the kit holding the repair items. He extracted a shiny new battery cable end and handed it to Vic. Vic stared at the tools and repair kit. He whistled low. "Dude. You are prepared."

"I hate sitting on the side of the road waiting for a tow." BB smirked a little to himself.

"I hear that." Vic took the part and the tools and started repairing the cable.

Officer Dewars continued to try to get information from Julie. "Do you know anyone who would want to prank you?"

"No."

The officer raised her eyebrows. "No one?"

"I said 'no.' I don't know anyone." Julie scowled and turned her back to the officer.

"What about someone who wants to hurt you?" Dewars continued to pursue the matter.

Julie's head snapped up. "How did we go from prank to hurt?"

Dewars shrugged. "If it's not a prank, then maybe the perpetrator wanted to strand you alone. So they could come by and pretend to help but with ill intent."

"Like these two clowns? I don't think so." Julie glared at BB and Vic.

Vic nudged BB. "That's the thanks we get for rescuing her."

BB snorted. "Yeah, I know. Happens a lot these days. Do something good and it blows up in your face."

Vic finished the repairs as Dewars completed her paperwork. Vic shut the hood with a solid "Whump." He wiped his hands on the towel BB offered him. The gridiron star smiled. "All fixed. You should be good to go."

BB suggested, "Try the engine."

Julie climbed behind the wheel, turned the key, and the engine purred to life. Julie nodded to Vic and BB. "Thank you. I appreciate the help." She had more than a note of sarcasm in her tone. Closer to a full chord.

Officer Dewars climbed into her buggy. "I'll see you back to your dorm. For safety's sake."

Julie's tone sounded anything but grateful. "Thanks. I appreciate the thought." She glared at BB. "We'll still get coffee."

BB nodded. "Tomorrow. In the daylight."

She turned and walked back to her dorm. BB watched until she entered the building, then faced Vic. "Thanks, man. You probably saved me."

Vic's eyes narrowed. "You owe me. Remember that."

BB's eyes went wide. Vic laughed. "Kidding. I'm joking. You don't owe me anything. I don't like seeing anyone taken advantage of. We still need to find Jamis' killer. I don't want to lose another friend."

BB listened carefully to Vic's words and filed them away for further examination. Under prayerful consideration. The two men slid into BB's car and drove back to their dorm. They climbed the stairs to their room and keyed their way in.

Leeland and Samuel were in their nightwear but were still sitting up. Waiting for Vic and BB, no doubt. Vic announced, "The cavalry returns. Unthanked but successful. The battery cable had been cut off. We fixed it."

Samuel sat up. "The battery cable had been cut?" His eyes flashed from Vic to BB and back to Vic.

BB nodded. "Yeah. Long story. Someone vandalized the car but only cut off the cable clamp. All while the car was locked. Nothing taken from the vehicle. Except the cable clamp."

Leeland snuffed. "That's a new one."

Vic added, "Security watched the whole repair. And escorted her back to her dorm. For safety. Handy people to have around."

Samuel chuckled. "Did Julie see it that way?"

BB answered for his roommate. "Not exactly. But she accepted it."

Samuel lost his levity. "You think she tried to bait you?" Samuel's eyes bored into BB.

BB took time to consider it. He hoped not. Sincerely hoped not. "I don't know. If she's working with Riley, maybe." He looked around the room. "I appreciate you guys keeping me out of trouble tonight."

Vic pulled on a nightshirt. "Forget it. You'd have done the same for me. We've got an early class. Call it a night."

BB followed Vic's lead, changed into his night clothes, then swung into his bunk. He lay awake and stared at the ceiling. *Lord, I was nearly a fool tonight. I didn't listen to Your Voice. Thank You for the counsel of my roommates. My friends. Lord, I think I see a change in Vic. Is that You? If not, change his heart. If it is You, continue to work on him so he admits You are in his life. Let me see it clearly. And thank You for all You're doing in this room. Only You could bring the changes I've seen. Help us find Jamis' killer. Or help the police find them. Bring the ones responsible to justice.*

BB closed his eyes. *Bless Dad and Wendy. Mom. Bless Ben and May and her mom, Aldi, Sassy, Chris and their mom. Bless Tav and Jen, Luke and Chay, Addison and Emma, Quinn and Grace, Whitney, Paul, Raymond, Tomas...* The list continued until BB fell asleep. And his sleep was peaceful.

* * *

THURSDAY

The text on BB's phone read, *Meet at Reclining Canine. Noon.*

Julie knew his schedule. He had no class at noon. Since the Canine was a public place and safe enough to meet at, he texted back, *See you there.* And made the call home.

Dad answered the phone. "BB. What's going on?" Dad sounded preoccupied.

"Checking on the family. What's Ben doing?"

"Resting."

"How is he as a patient?"

"So far, no complaints. We have an appointment on Tuesday for the orthopedist to look at his shoulder. They'll decide what to do then."

"Do they set a collar bone?"

"I don't think so, but I'm not the expert. We'll see on Wednesday."

"What's mom doing?"

"She's making cookies to take to Mr. Hardaway. A thank-you for helping Ben."

"What about you??" Hard to know what his dad would be into in the middle of the day.

"Avoiding work. I need to review the tax statements for my newest client, but they're such a mess I don't want to continue. So I thought I'd attack the oleanders again. Work out some aggression."

BB chuckled. "You know they fight back."

"I've noticed. Anything I can help you with?"

BB hesitated, then said, "I need prayer. I'm seeing Julie this afternoon. I need to be clear whether she's working for me or against me."

"Oh?" Dad's voice rose several notes.

"Yeah." BB drew in a deep breath. "Here's the deal." He explained the incident the night before and his questions about Julie.

Dad listened. "Are you sure meeting her is a good idea?"

"I'll be careful, Dad. We're still near campus. And it's the middle of the day. What—"

"Do not say 'what could happen?' It's too much like a challenge to the cosmos. Take backup. Always take backup."

BB's shoulders dropped. He knew Dad would say that. Knew it. "I hear you, Dad. I said I'll be careful. I will."

"Call me when you're done."

"Yes, sir."

"We're praying for you."

"Love you, Dad." BB disconnected the call. He made one more text and headed to his mid-morning class. The last physics class before he would meet Julie. The last one before…

Focus. One day at a time. One hour at a time. Right. One hour. BB marched on.

* * *

THURSDAY NOON

Just before noon, BB pulled into the parking lot at the *Reclining Canine*. Julie's car sat near the front. BB noticed there were a handful of vehicles besides hers present. He parked, got out, and strolled into the restaurant.

Julie sat at the back in a booth. She wore a black leather jacket against the spring chill. The young woman faced the front so she could watch for BB. She waved as he passed the "Please be seated" sign.

The restaurant was about half-full. BB had expected there to be more people at lunch. It wasn't a place where you needed reservations. He eyed the room without appearing to do so. Two women sat in the booth opposite Julie's table. Both looked a little wild and unkempt, but hey, a paying patron is a dollar earned. The rest of the customers were either on the patio or across the room.

Julie rose as he approached, leaned out, and hugged him. Warmly. Too warmly.

BB broke it off and slid to the side opposite her. "Hi." Keep it simple and above board.

Julie's lower lip stuck out as she sat down, but she responded in kind. "Hi."

BB admitted, "I've been here but only for the dessert menu. What's good?"

"Burgers are standard. The Reuben is to die for, the French Dip is heavenly, and the open-face meatloaf sandwich is just like Mama would have made…if she could cook."

BB grinned. "I wouldn't know."

"Neither did Mama. I'm having the chipotle beef salad."

BB picked up the laminated menu, wiped the dampness off of it, and perused the offerings. After a few moments, he decided and looked up at Julie. "I'll have the French Dip."

"Good choice. Most things here are a good choice. Which is why we're here. Good food, good company…" Her eyes narrowed slightly. "Good conversation."

BB pursed his lips but smiled with his eyes. *Stay non-committal until you know what she's driving at.* As if he couldn't guess.

The server came, took their orders, brought their drinks, and then disappeared. Julie shook out her napkin and placed it in her lap. BB glanced at the beer and wine menu, turned it upside down, and set it back in its place. He took in a slow, deep breath, exhaled, and asked, "You want to talk about it now or wait for the food?"

"Oh, let's wait. Why ruin a good lunch?"

BB studied her face. He could read little in her eyes. Bemusement, maybe? A tinge of something he couldn't put his finger on. He would proceed with caution. Keep it light where he could. "How are classes going?"

"Psych is driving me crazy. I can't keep all the maladies straight. And Advanced Algebra is ridiculous. I wish I'd paid more attention in high school." Julie swirled her glass to make the ice in her cola rotate. She tipped her head. "You're in physics. That means you've taken trig, right?"

"Yeah." This was a nice, safe topic of conversation. Though she had expressed her frustration with math before. That part must be real in her life.

"Then can you help me with studying?"

"I might be able to help you. When? The library is open

until nine most nights. Except on weekends."

"My dorm room is open all the time." Julie smiled over her glass.

BB shook his head. "Unless we meet downstairs in the common area, it's a no."

Julie shrugged. "Didn't hurt to ask. Just wanted to see if your answer had changed."

"It won't."

The young woman held his eyes. "I didn't think it would. But I had to try."

"Why?"

The server brought the dishes. BB prayed silently over his food. He placed his napkin on his lap. It promptly slipped to the floor. He and Julie took big bites of their respective meals in time for the server to return and ask, "Is everything all right?"

"Mmhm." BB nodded. Julie gave the server a thumbs-up. BB swallowed his food and asked, "Can you bring me another napkin? I dropped mine on the floor."

The server smiled, "Of course, sir," then gave the necessary, "If you need anything, call me," and departed. BB reached down, gathered the wayward cloth, and stuck it in his pocket. He'd put it on the table when they were done.

They finished several more bites before Julie came back to the conversation. "You asked why. I wanted to learn how important I might be to you. If I were important enough you'd come to see me in my room."

The server slipped by and laid another napkin on BB's side of the table. BB shook it out and placed it in his lap. The spare, he kept in his pocket.

BB swallowed the food in his mouth and chose his words carefully. "You are important to me, Julie. I like you. But I can't go to your room. We established that fact in the beginning. I'm pledged to the Lord and will follow what He says in Scripture."

Julie leaned forward and pointed her fork at him. "Show

me in Scripture where Jesus specifically says, 'BB, don't go to Julie's room.' You can't." She sat back with a satisfied smirk.

BB didn't change tones. He remained calm and reasonable. "I can show you where the Apostle Paul told Timothy to 'flee youthful lust.'"

Julie's jaw dropped slightly. "So, you've lusted after me? How flattering."

BB shook his head. "The command is to prevent lust, not allow it to happen, then run away. Running away comes before the lust can begin."

"But the night we were at the mall, you kissed me."

"And I shouldn't have." BB lowered his head, stared at his plate, and raised his head again. "I like you, Julie. We could be friends. I can help you with your studies. But I'm not getting romantically involved. I can't."

Julie's tone arched with her eyebrows. "Can't? Or won't?"

"Won't. Can't. Either way you want to look at it. I serve the Lord." He found comfort in declaring the commitment. A rock to stand on.

"And he's more important than anyone else." Disgust laced her tone.

"Yes." Lay it out there without apology. "He's first in my life. Period."

"You wouldn't bend your morals to help a friend? Or save their life?"

"What are you talking about—save their life?" BB narrowed his focus. Studying her face. Her body language. Where did she intend to go with this?

Julie toyed with the lettuce in her salad. She looked up at BB and admitted, "I'm in trouble. I'm supposed to entice you to come to Riley Crimmons' soiree. She'll get me into real deep water if I don't succeed. She wants you to escort her pledges. You'd be perfect."

BB shook his head. "I've already told her no."

Julie snorted. "And you see what it got you. Your church robbed. Your pastor attacked."

The muscles in BB's arms tightened. Calm. He would remain calm. "Riley Crimmons set up the attack on Pastor Dee?"

Julie shook her head. "You never made the connection? Of course, she did. It was her way of warning you to get in line."

"And the smear of my name?" How twisted…could this really be happening? BB's jaw dropped.

"When you didn't take the first hint, she had to get serious." Julie shrugged as if it made perfect sense.

BB's gut twisted. How sick— Only one problem with this. One hole in her story. "But what did Jamis do? How did he cross her?"

Julie shrugged. "I heard he committed suicide and blamed Vic. Vic is scum. He deserves to live with a guilty conscience."

BB played his ace. "Except it wasn't suicide. I have proof."

Julie's face darkened. "What?"

"Proof his death was premeditated murder. I'm on the way to the police as soon as we're done here."

Julie lowered her eyes and stabbed a piece of beef. She chewed it, swallowed, then asked, "What proof could you possibly have? If the police say it was suicide, how could you have anything different?"

BB sat back from the table. "I tracked down the rumors about Jamis and me. Three of them were started before the police say Jamis died. How could anyone know about his death when it hadn't happened yet?"

Julie shrugged. "Maybe the people who heard the rumor got the time wrong."

"They were quite adamant about the hour. Told me what they were watching live on the 'net. I tracked down the times. They knew before Jamis was killed." BB toyed with the drink menu. He laid it on the table flat.

"And you're on the way to tell the police?"

"After we're done here. Someone has to tell them. With what the police already have, they will make the case for murder easily." *Get it all out there, and she'll reciprocate. They could end the farce.*

Julie mixed the greens in her dish, searching for more beef. She found a piece, chewed it, then asked, "What do they have? And how do you know about it?"

BB took a long drink of his cola. "I read the reports. Don't ask how I got hold of them. I know a guy who knows a guy." He smiled a straight-lipped smile. "I also talked to people who knew him. The police report says he had a gunshot wound to his heart. Men who kill themselves don't aim for their chest. Too difficult to hold the gun. No, they shoot themselves in the head." BB swallowed hard. He hadn't wanted to share everything he knew about suicide. He certainly wasn't going to tell her where he'd learned it. Dad's depression remained ongoing. He had a handle on it, but life was a "one day at a time" battle for him. And yet another reason Dad walked so close to the Lord. Christ stayed his source of life, the One Rock on which he could stand.

BB went on. "I talked with Jamis' family. They all knew he was out. He knew they knew. There was no secret. The letter was meant to hurt Vic. It did a good job of it, too." He scowled. Yes, good had come of it. But it didn't justify the damage done. "Jamis deserves better." *So do I.*

He asked his final question. "How much did you know about this?" He pushed his empty bowl and plate away.

Julie shoved the salad away. "Is that why you agreed to come? To see if I knew about Jamis' death?" Her calm confidence slipped.

"Is that why you asked me? To see what I knew?" He tossed her accusation back at her.

"To see if you knew. Riley said you were pushing for

answers. That the rumor tree had become hot with inquiries." Julie reached into her jacket pocket. She kept her hands under the table.

BB held Julie's eyes. "Who killed him? Riley? Or you?"

"If you don't know, why should I tell you?" Julie smirked. Triumph burned in her eyes.

BB remained calm and purposeful. "Because you pulled a gun, and you're aiming to march me out of here. Maybe kill me too. You might as well tell me."

The smirk deepened. "Why don't we let the police figure it out?" The sarcasm seemed forced.

BB let a slow smile cross his face. "What's the fun in doing that? The perpetrator always tells the victim what they want to know. It's the rules."

Julie snorted. "And you always follow the rules." BB read the slightest hint of fear in her eyes. Fear, but determination as well. She would kill him, given the chance.

But in a restaurant full of people? In broad daylight? She had to have a plan of escape. Or else…

BB kept this voice even. "How did you get in so deep? What does Riley Crimmons have on you?" Let her talk. He needed whatever information he could get to make this make sense.

"On me?" Julie laughed. "She has nothing 'on' me. I want something from her. Her fine old family buys and sells influence. Politics. Academia. Medicine. You name it, they have a hand in it. And a reach over it. Connections. It's not just a game people play. It's what life is all about. Hook up with her, and I can have anything I want."

BB asked the obvious. "And when she decides she's done with you? Then what?"

"I still have the connections. She can't shut them all down. I'm still on top."

Still, there remained one hole. "But why Jamis?"

Julie shook her head. "Show of force. Example to others. She wanted Jamis for her escort service. He dissed her like you did. But three times. If word got out people could refuse her, where would her power be? He had to go. Killing him and blaming it on you proved the easy out."

The young woman—the assassin?—lifted the gun high enough above the table so BB could see it. "Let's go. We're going to walk out of here nice and slow. We're going to get in your car, and you're going to take us on a country drive."

"Won't fly, Julie. No one who knows me will believe I went somewhere with you alone. Can't happen. The police will be all over that lie."

She smiled. "I can be very persuasive. Move."

He stalled. "Shouldn't we wait for the bill? Leaving without paying is a fast way to be exposed."

Julie's eyes flared. She sat back in the seat. "Why are you warning me? It's like you want me to take you out." The hand holding the gun never wavered.

BB fingered the drink menu. "I don't want anyone else to get hurt. You might get nervous and trigger-happy if they stop us at the door. I don't think you've done anything like this before."

Julie narrowed her eyes. "You think you're so smooth. You don't know what I'm capable of."

"I'm going to find out, aren't I?" BB set the menu back in its place, still upside down. He flagged down the server. "Check, please."

The server nodded and walked away. BB eyed Julie. "You didn't kill Jamis. Riley did."

Julie lifted her head. "I'm happy you don't think I'm a murderer. You're wrong, but I'm glad you didn't think it was me. I do like you, BB."

"Did Riley come up with that idea, too? Who initiated the romance angle?"

"No. Enticing you was my idea. I thought maybe if you saw the advantages, you'd come around. But you never bent your morals." She pursed her lips and let out a small sigh. "Not even for me."

"Not for anyone." I'm not asking for a test, Lord. Beyond this one.

Julie clicked her tongue and shook her head. "You'll never find a girl that way, you know."

BB made sure to keep his hands on the tabletop. "If I have to compromise who I am and Who I serve, it's not meant to be."

The server returned with their ticket. BB pulled out a credit card. "On me." The server ran it, handed the card and receipt to BB, and left.

Julie closed her eyes for a moment. "Gallant to the last. I can't stand it." She stood. "Let's go."

BB slid out of his chair. He dropped the unused napkin on the table.

The two women in the booth exited at the same time. One of them wobbled as she walked. Unstable. Drunk? Maybe. BB watched her stumble against Julie as Julie cleared the corner of the table.

Julie moved to push the woman off, but the drunken woman reached out to steady herself. In one smooth motion, she grabbed Julie's gun hand. She shoved the gun toward the floor.

Julie screamed in frustration. She fought to retain possession of the gun, but the intruder proved stronger. BB stepped back to stay out of the possible line of fire and not interfere with the takedown.

There was no question of the outcome. The woman had years of training on her side. Julie had nothing. In a moment it ended, as the woman twisted the gun free of Julie's hand. The woman grinned evilly at Julie. "Sorry, honey, but you'll only hurt yourself with this."

Julie screamed again, "Someone help me! I'm being kidnapped! They've got a gun!"

The woman reached into her shirt and pulled out an ID and a badge. She held the badge high and called out, "City police. Everyone stay where you are. Everything is under control here."

The manager walked over to the table. He stuttered only a little as he reported, "The police are on their way."

The woman smiled. "My backup. Always running late." She smiled at BB. "Nice work using the signals with the menu. You did it perfectly. Almost like you knew what you were doing."

BB smiled at Tamara. "I appreciate you being here."

Julie glared from BB to Tamara. "You two set this up." It was an accusation, not a question.

BB nodded. "I hoped it wouldn't go down this way. I really hoped you weren't part of this. But I had to know. And I had to be prepared."

Julie spit at him. "Boy Scout."

BB used the extra napkin to wip the spit from his shirt. "You don't have to take the fall for Riley, you know. You can come clean and work with the DA. It would look better for you."

Julie snorted. "What will look better is me being a good soldier and staying the course. Good soldiers get rewarded."

Tamara shook her head. "Little girl, you don't have a clue how many 'good soldiers' we've put away while the Crimmons family goes on living the high life. They are only loyal to themselves, no one else. They'll cut you off like they have all the others." Tamara interrupted Julie's attempt to speak. "And don't tell me you're different. She owes you nothing. And that's what you'll get from her. Nothing. I'll show you the roster when we get downtown."

Tamara handcuffed Julie and walked her out of the restaurant. BB caught the manager before the man could reach the front desk. His nametag read Tom. BB said, "I'm sorry she had to choose your place to make her stand. But I appreciate all your help with keeping me alive."

The manager's voice shook as he nodded and said, "You're welcome. I'm glad we could be of service to the police."

BB tried to smile. "I'll be sure to send all my friends down this way. The food is great." He stopped. "The company left something to be desired, but the food is great." He slipped the man a check. "This should cover any of your lost revenue."

Tom glanced at the amount of the check and looked up at BB with his jaw hanging open. "We've never done that much business in a day, much less two hours. Are you sure?"

BB nodded. "Keep it anonymous. And have a good day."

Tom bobbed his head up and down as he pumped BB's hand. "Absolutely. Absolutely, I will. And you, too."

BB walked out of the door. He went to his car, climbed in, closed the door, then put his head on the steering wheel and breathed out a long, slow sigh. He sat that way for several moments until a knock on his window startled him. He looked up.

Popdad Quinn stood at the door, waiting for BB to roll down his window. BB opened the door instead. He got out and hugged his granddad. All the tension and fear and anxiety poured out into the embrace.

When he came back to himself, he stepped away from Quinn. "How did you know to be here?"

Stocky, compact, but muscular, the silver-haired man laughed. "I have connections. Your roommates told me. I showed up at your dorm, and they were more than happy to tell me where you'd gone. They were concerned about you."

BB chuckled silently. "Nice to have friends who care."

"I heard you were having problems with that bunch." Quinn eyed BB as he motioned for him to sit.

BB sat back in the driver's seat but left his legs outside the car. "Those guys? Nah. They're a great bunch. We had a few misunderstandings in the beginning, but we worked it out." BB stopped, then admitted, "The Lord worked it out."

Quinn smiled. "He usually does when we let Him."

"I'm learning, Popdad. I'm learning."

Quinn shoved BB's shoulder. "Food any good in here?"

"Excellent. Highly recommended."

Quinn stretched. "Well, think I'll stop in for lunch. I wasn't spying on you. I just came for the food."

BB grinned. "Thanks, Popdad. Love you, too."

"Go to school."

"Yes, sir." BB slid back into the driver's position, started the car, and headed to his dorm. He had some friends waiting. Good friends. And maybe a brother in the Lord. *Thank You, Lord. Move on Julie's heart. Bring the others to You as well. In Your precious Name I pray, amen.*

The motor purred.

* * *

EPILOGUE

BB and Ben sat on the bench outside the dorm. The air smelled fine, the day warm. Half a dozen students were splayed out on the grounds, lying on blankets, towels, or the grass itself. The sun shone high in the sky, strong enough for the first semblance of a tan if BB had been so inclined.

Which he wasn't. Ben was talking, explaining about how he and Tricia had spent spring break. "Since I still can't use my arm, she's been helping with May. Since the police cleared you, she's back. Tricia loves helping Mom with May. She treats her like a baby doll. Always dressing her up in these crazy outfits. I think Mom is having fun with her. Maybe she sees Tricia as a daughter. Or another woman to talk to. Mom says all the testosterone gets to be a little much at times."

BB laughed. "Yeah, I can see why. Men do outnumber the women in the Knights."

"At the house, too. Mialma doesn't really count as another woman."

"No, she doesn't. What does Tricia's mom think about her being over at the house?"

"She's happy Tricia has a safe place to be. She's gotten to know Mom and Dad, so she likes Tricia being somewhere she can find her." Ben looked up at BB. Ben seemed lost in thought, then blurted out, "You lost your girlfriend."

"My friend. Julie wasn't a girlfriend like you mean. Not that one special friend. She couldn't be."

"Because she didn't follow Jesus? Or because she wanted to kill you?"

BB stretched his arms across the top of the bench and laughed. "Well, wanting to kill me was definitely a red flag. But no, you're right. She didn't follow Jesus. We could never be serious if she didn't."

Ben chewed on his lip. "But can you be serious with someone who wants to learn about Jesus? Who maybe hasn't asked Him into their heart, but is thinking about it?"

BB hesitated. "What happens if they don't ever accept Him? Then what?"

Ben stared at the ground. He looked up and said, "I guess that would be bad."

"It could be. Scriptures tell us not to be 'unequally yoked.' When the Scripture was written, it talked about hooking up an ox and a donkey to pull a wagon. The ox is big and strong, and the donkey isn't. The ox will pull the load, the donkey will make the ox work harder, and the wagon won't get where it needs to go. Jesus didn't tell us not to be unequal because He wanted to take away our choices. He wants to protect us from being in a bad situation."

"Tricia doesn't know Jesus. Should I be friends with her?"

"Of course you should. You should be friends with everyone. How will you show anyone the love of Christ if you're not their friend? Jesus didn't say don't be friends with people who don't know Him. He said don't get closely hooked together."

Ben shook his head. "I like Tricia."

"That's a good thing. But you're too young to have a steady girlfriend. You don't know enough about the birds and bees to be making a life choice."

"And you do?"

Did BB detect sarcasm in Ben's retort? BB smiled. "No, I don't, either. I haven't found the right person."

A voice yelled across the commons. BB looked up and saw Vic and Leeland walking toward them. BB waved. "I'll introduce you to my roommates. Well, two of them, anyhow."

"Are these the guys who were giving you a hard time? Being mean to you? Blowing smoke in your face?"

BB smiled. "Yes, they were. But all that's in the past. They helped me track down Julie as the suspect. And Vic has been asking questions about Jesus. He won't tell me if he's accepted Him or not, but his actions sure show a difference."

Ben nodded. "It's easy to say you follow Jesus. It's harder to do it."

"Yeah, but Vic's got a good start."

Leeland and Vic approached the bench. BB stood, as did Ben. Vic's face shone from some inner light. He extended his hand. "BB! Haven't seen you since spring break. How you doing?"

"Great." BB hugged Vic, then Leeland. "What are you two up to?"

"Getting ready for the fall term. Got my schedule today."

Ben asked, "What are you taking?"

Vic looked at Ben in confusion. BB made the introductions. "Guys, my brother, Ben."

Vic nodded. "Ah…the B of BB. I've heard good things about you."

Ben lowered his eyes. BB bumped him on the shoulder. Ben raised his eyes and met Vic's. "Thank you."

Leeland extended his fist. Ben bumped it. Leeland laughed. "Always good to see family. If you got 'em, flaunt 'em."

BB repeated Ben's question. "What classes will you have?"

Vic smiled. "I'm looking into business in case the

football doesn't pan out."

Leeland shook his head. "I'm still undeclared. I haven't made up my mind."

Vic's eyes glinted. "Have to have a mind to make up first."

Leeland bumped Vic. Vic retaliated. BB decided to step in before it became a free-for-all. "Where were you guys heading?"

"Cafeteria. Gotta get there before all the good food is gone." Leeland laughed.

Vic grumbled if only a little. "None of it is. But it's food."

Ben eyed BB. BB read his intent, but asked, "Sure?" Ben nodded. BB turned to his roommates. "I'm taking Ben out for dinner. You two want to join us?" BB chuckled. "But you two, not the whole team."

A faint color filled Vic's cheeks. He recovered quickly, however. "Naw, it's bro time. I understand."

Ben shook his head. "Honest. I'd like you to come. I want to get to know the men my brother rooms with. I want to find out what makes a good roommate." His face drew down into his "serious" look. "For when I go to college."

As the four walked to the parking lot, Vic offered, "Respect. Courtesy. Communication. We all have it for each other. That's what makes it work."

Leeland added, "Yeah. Not leaving your dirty laundry for someone else to pick up or trip over."

"Not blaring your music unless by mutual consent," Vic commented.

"Choosing music everyone can agree on," Leeland threw in his take on it.

"Compromise. Being willing to compromise on everything but the essentials."

BB listened and smiled. Inside. Who were these guys, and what had they done with his roommates? *This is all You, Lord. Only You. Thank You. And don't let me mess it up.* BB kept his face straight. "Do tell. What else?"

Vic grinned. "Oh, you know. All the things we taught you when the semester started. You were so green. We had to teach you everything."

BB shook his head. "Let's go, reprobates." He grinned.

If you enjoyed ***Knights of the Octagon,*** sign up for Colleen Snyder's newsletter to keep up with new books and projects. It will also give you a place to talk to the author directly. And she loves to talk to her readers. Trust me!
Emails will NOT be sold, shared, or used for any other purpose. Promise.
Go to: **colleensnyderauthor.com** and leave your email to sign up.
Also connect with her at Facebook, **Colleen K. Snyder, Author.**

Did you miss the first books in the Knights of the Octagon Series? Find them here:

Knights of the Octagon: Benefactor
Book I
It's life or death. Can they pull together to survive?
Dumped from a raft in the middle of God literally only knows where, four friends are stranded in the wilderness. No cellphones. No maps. No food. Three pocket knives, a compass, and each other are all they have.
Until two shadowy figures lead Micah and his friends to a stash of survival equipment scrounged from the river. Who are these mysterious benefactors? What do they want?
Then rescue comes with a catch. Micah and his friends can wait four days to be taken to civilization or join a real-life quest for a million dollars. The Magary treasure hunt—going on its fiftieth year with no winners—has seen deaths before. With a murderer in the field, will the men become victims?
Is the reward worth the risk? Can the Knights work as a team to not only survive but find a treasure no one else has found?
Where is God in their search? In their lives?
Join the Knights of the Octagon on their first adventure.

Also find

<u>Knights of the Octagon: MIA</u>
<u>BOOK II</u>
Q is missing.
Quinn Magary, patron, supporter, champion of the Knights of the
Octagon, is missing.
Five days late from a three-day personal assignment, and no one
can find him.
Then Grace Painter, another member of the Knights, disappears
without warning.
The remaining Knights—Tav, Luke, and Micah—vow to find
their friends and mentors.
Then someone runs Tav off the road. And Micah is nearly
murdered at Grace Painter's worksite. An innocent lunch date
becomes a conflagration as a shadowy figure blows up the
restaurant.

Dead bodies appear. Knights are battered, kidnapped, and left for dead. Who is after them? Why? What can they do to end the attacks? And above all, where are Quinn and Grace?

MIA

<u>Knights of the Octagon: Quake</u>
BOOK III
The Quake is Coming

Impeccable research from a brave geologist predicts a major earthquake for the local area. Soon. Within thirty days soon. Not all his colleagues agree with his conclusions. The quake is coming? Absolutely. But three weeks? More like three years. Maybe.

A group of young men are convinced of the geologist's calculations. They're preparing for it. Frantically buying food and supplies for the survivors. But will there be any? Of the five thousand people in town, how many will believe their report? "Orton's Crazies," people call them. "Cultists" who want to sit on a hilltop and wait for the end to come.

It would be easier for the Knights not to tell anyone and simply get out of town. But then how many deaths will be on their heads? How do you convince people—family, friend, and foe alike—of a truth they don't want to hear??
The quake is coming. What would you do about it?

<u>Knights of the Octagon: Wedding Crasher</u>

Book IV
The masked figure poured accelerant over the sparkling dreams, wishes, and hopes. Chemicals melted delicate lace tulle. The liquid scarred the shimmering satins. Pearl buttons dissolved. The flash of ignition turned yards of fabric to ash.

An arsonist is destroying wedding shops. Vandalizing event centers, flower warehouses, and anything wedding-related. But it's still "only" vandalism. Until Micah Andres and Wendy Smothers are taste-testing cakes for their upcoming wedding. An SUV demolishes the building. The baker is killed.

Now it's murder, and mayhem ensues…

The van Micah is riding in is hit with bullets. The county

office he is visiting is blown up. Someone firebombs the houses where the Knights live. Is this the arsonist? Or is something deeper going on? Can Micah and the Knights find out before the murderer strikes again?

Join the *Knights of the Octagon* in their adventure: *Wedding Crasher*.

<u>Knights of the Octagon: The Christmas Stalker</u>
BOOK V
I can't wait to be with you. Friday can't come soon enough.
Chay Waylon is receiving threatening messages from her own email account. Someone is mimicking her address. Someone who wants more than her attention. He's pursuing an imaginary relationship. A Christmas romance.
But why? And most important, who?
Ken, her boss, thinks she's sending the messages to herself to

create drama. No big deal. Get back to work.

Then, the entire office system is locked out with Chay's picture on every screen throughout the accounting company. Ransom is demanded. Ken is convinced Chay is behind the theft.

How can she clear her name of the holiday hoax and catch the stalker who wants to make her his own?

And when the once love of her life makes a second appearance, will she let him go again? Or will she admit she needs help and welcome him back in her life…this time forever?

ABOUT THE AUTHOR

Colleen K. Snyder has always had a passion for writing. She authored two previously published books: *Journey to Amanah: The Beginning* and *Return to Tebel-Ayr: The Journey Continues* (B&H Publishing). In 2020 she published the first book in the *Collin Walker* series: *Verdict at the River's Edge*. There are now seven books in the series. She lives on a "ranchette" in California and is the juniorest ranch hand. She serves on her church prayer team, and exercises a ministry of intercessory prayer. She has worked as a factory line worker, pharmacy technician, USAF missile systems analyst, janitor, nanny, teacher, accounting manager and anything else the Lord required. Her son, Bear and his wife Krystal, their two daughters, Mara and Kaylynn, and her daughter Katie all live in Ohio.

Colleen's story is for His glory, always.

Read on to learn more about Colleen's books in the *Collin Walker* series.

The Collin Walker Series

Seven books of action and suspense for your reading enjoyment. Follow Collin Walker as she follows the Lord into murder, intrigue, mayhem…you know, Life.
Available on Kindle, KindleUnlimited, and in paperback.
(Also hardback, but why??)

www.ingramcontent.com/pod-product-compliance
Lightning Source LLC
Chambersburg PA
CBHW070419310726
48977CB00003B/751